Return to My Village in the Valley

ALSO BY MICHAEL BARTLETT

SHORT STORY COLLECTIONS

MY VILLAGE IN THE VALLEY

PERSONAL ISLANDS

A DIFFERENT DRUM

NOVELS

DREAMS OF ELEVEN

HUNTING THE HORNETS

Crumps Barn Studio
Syde, Cheltenham GL53 9PN
www.crumpsbarnstudio.co.uk

Copyright © Michael Bartlett 2024

The right of Michael Bartlett to be identified as the author of this work has been asserted in accordance with the Copyright, Designs and Patents Act 1988.

All rights reserved. No part of this publication may be reproduced, stored in a retrieval system, or transmitted in any form or by any means, electronic, mechanical, photocopying, recording or otherwise, without the prior permission of the copyright owner.

Cover design by Lorna Gray

Typeset in Adobe Garamond Pro

All our books are printed on responsibly sourced paper from managed woodlands. Printed in the UK by CMP, Poole.

ISBN 978-1-915067-56-2

MICHAEL BARTLETT

Return to My Village in the Valley

Never underestimate a quiet little country backwater ...

Crumps Barn Studio

A note from the author:

As I said in the original *'My Village In The Valley'*, these stories are not about the village I live in. My fictional village has a pub and a shop and the village I live in has neither so that proves it.

However I would like to thank my many friends in Norfolk and Suffolk villages, with special thanks to Joy who (unwittingly) inspired one story and to Sue who taught me (theoretically) how to ride a cow.

I should also mention my dad, Alf Bartlett, who first created the fairies in 1931.

There Ain't No Place Like Gnome

My Village in the Valley is a quiet unassuming place where, on the whole, very little happens. My neighbours are a broad mix. Some, like me, were born in the village. Some, unlike me, have families which go back generations here. Some are incomers, from elsewhere in the county or from further afield, but most have been absorbed into village life and we don't take kindly to outsiders telling us what to do.

So when Nan Mildew had a letter from our District Council ordering her to remove the gnomes in her front garden we all rallied round. True, most of us were not enamoured of the garish coloured gnomes themselves but we didn't see why officialdom should ban them. The letter, which came from Melvin Turtlebong, a local council Planning Officer, stated that the gnomes were causing harm to the character and setting of a listed building and must be removed with immediate effect.

Several of the cottages and other buildings in our village are Grade II listed, which mostly means that the outside of the building must be kept looking much as it always has done. If the window frames are made of wood, then they must be replaced with wood, and with the same number of panes of glass. This rarely causes controversy as very few people would want to bash a hole in the front wall of an 1870s cottage and install picture windows in UPVC.

Even so there are occasional spats. When Sylvia wanted to install double glazed windows in her 1890 cottage she was told that double glazing was not allowed in a listed building. She challenged that but got nowhere until her builder had a word with the District Council's Chief Executive. When they looked at the detailed regulations together they discovered that, while it was compulsory to install double glazing in any new build, it was optional – not forbidden – in a listed building. So Sylvia got her double glazing.

Back to Nan's gnomes. As always when there were off-the-record village matters to discuss, a meeting was held in The Spy. The proper name of our village pub is *The One-Armed Spyglass*, an obscure name to many people until they realise that the reference is to Nelson who had connections with this county. In fact Nelson never came near our village and we're a long way from the sea, but the naming of English pubs has always defied logic.

There was quite a crowd in The Spy that night. My usual circle of drinking companions, Harry, Sylvia, Bill, Jessica and Nigel were all there of course, but we were joined by Emery Jacobs, our curate Bev the Rev, Sunita Devi, Silas Pring, Pawel Adamski, Ronald Trigg, and Marjorie Fawcett.

The general view was that Nan Mildew's gnomes, while not being exactly objects of beauty, were causing no harm to anyone and the Council had no right to insist they be removed.

"Does anyone actually know what the listed building

planning regulations say?" asked Bev the Rev.

"Not in detail," said Harry, "but I find it hard to believe they single out gnomes in particular."

"Nan showed me the letter" said Marjorie, "there was a lot of guff about appropriate objects within the curtilage of a traditional building, and the gnomes marring the townscape and affecting the view. Load of old cobblers."

Marjorie is Chairman of the Parish Council and is notorious for her contempt for 'jobsworth' officialdom.

"What about those two gnomes bending over, one above the other," said Bill, "they are a bit suggestive."

"Nan insists they're bending over to pick the flowers," said Harry.

We all looked at each other. We had all, separately, come to a different conclusion about what the gnomes were doing. However, the point was that Nan was upset, for no good reason as far as we could see, so something had to be done about it.

With such a diverse population in my Village in the Valley we can usually pinpoint someone to help sort out any problems and in this case the spotlight fell on Nigel.

Nigel is a retired solicitor. He has only lived in the village for about three years but he rapidly became an integral part of our village life.

During his first year here, he asked Rupert to teach him how to use a shotgun, which Rupert was happy to do but asked why he wanted to learn as he didn't see Nigel as a natural for country pursuits.

Nigel's reply endeared him to us all. "Well, what I thought was, if I am ever diagnosed with a terminal disease I could blow the head off someone who has spent all their life making people's lives a misery and so feel I had finally done something useful with my life."

He beamed round at us all then added, "I have a list of possible contenders which I constantly keep up to date."

He didn't specify what sort of people were on his list, and we couldn't determine how serious he was, but we liked his attitude.

As so often with discussions in The Spy the outcome of the gnome conference was that something must be done, we just weren't too clear on what the 'something' would be. That Gordian Knot was cut by Sunita, ever the voice of common sense.

"Surely someone needs to go and see Nan," she said, "have a closer look at these gnomes and see where we go from there."

There was a pause and we all turned to look at Nigel who sighed.

"Okay," he said, "I'll go but I want someone to come with me in case she gets stroppy."

In the end it was me who went with Nigel on the gnome fact-finding expedition and it was a bit of eye-opener. Nan certainly had a lot of gnomes but there was more to it than that. When we got there we learned that the gnomes had actually been made for her by her grandson who ran a small pottery from his home in a village just over the county border. She had told him what she wanted and he had obliged, which made the gnomes even more personal.

"I don't see what be wrong with me gnomes," said Nan, "they bain't be doing no harm to no-one. And what's all this about a 'kurty ledge'? I don't have no kurty ledge."

"Don't you worry, Nan," said Nigel, "we'll get this sorted."

As this was a District Council matter Nigel decided to start with our local District Councillor, Katherine Warburton. None of us knew Katherine very well. Her predecessor, Kevin Tinker, had actually lived in our village and had been as much use as a chocolate fireguard. A smarmy man, "All mouth and no trousers," as Rupert put it. When he lost his council seat, which was won by Katherine, he moved out of the village and was not missed.

Anyway, Nigel contacted Katherine and suggested she come for a drink in The Spy one night as there were "a couple of local matters" that we would like to discuss with her. She was more than happy to meet a few more of her constituents so along she came, accepted a dry white wine and smiled round at us all.

"Good to meet you," she said, "I've been trying to get round the local villages in my patch but it all takes time." She glanced round the bar. "I should have made this village a priority. What a lovely pub."

That got us off on the right foot and so we proceeded to tell her about Nan's gnomes. She was clearly a bit nonplussed.

"Well, that I wasn't expecting," she said, "usually people want to talk to me about overgrown footpaths or cancelled bus routes."

"Well, as you have raised the issue …" Pawel began but we cut him short.

"Nor now, Pawel," said Jessica, "let's concentrate on the gnomes."

"The thing is, Katherine, can you help us sort this out?"

said Nigel. "Those gnomes are very dear to Nan's heart. Her grandson made them for her specially."

"Well, I can certainly try," said Katherine, "I think the best thing is for me to go and see these gnomes for myself."

"No problem," said Nigel, "let's find a convenient time and I'll take you over there."

Katherine finished her wine and ordered another round, something else that endeared her to us. Kevin Tinker wouldn't have given you the clippings from his toe nails.

"I'll need to read up on the listed building regs," said Katherine, "but I'm pretty sure that they don't mention gnomes."

"I bet they don't," said Harry.

"The only possible snag is …"

We glanced at each other. It had all seemed to be going so smoothly.

"… the current Senior Planning Officer. I happen to know he is very buddy-buddy with Melvin Turtlebong and if Melvin gets stroppy, well, we could have a problem."

We left it at that but our level of optimism had fallen. We'd all had experience of how obstructive our District Council could be. It's such a shame. Some things they do brilliantly. The refuse collection services – rubbish bins, recycling bins, garden waste – are all run efficiently and the council workers on the truck are unfailingly cheerful. If the village hall wants to run an event which requires a TEN, a Temporary Events Notice, all that is required is a phone call followed up by an email giving the date and details. The response will always be quick and courteous.

And yet … and yet … There was the time the District

Council gave its backing to a huge supermarket development on the edge of the village, a proposal so universally unpopular that at first we could not believe they were serious. But they were. Ignoring all local protests they planned to go ahead and it was only because of a nifty piece of guerilla action – and a bit of massaging of the truth – by determined villagers that they were finally stopped.

With that experience behind us we were not confident about a sensible solution to the gnome problem, but we agreed it was worth giving it a go.

A few days later Katherine, Nigel and I went to see Nan Mildew. Katherine was rather taken aback by the size and number of the gnomes, and when she saw the two gnomes bending over, she did raise an eyebrow. Nevertheless, she repeated that in her view the gnomes did not contravene listed building regulations.

Unfortunately the Senior Planning Officer did not agree. Private meetings between him and Katherine were inconclusive and the matter went to a full meeting of the planning committee. The vote there was a close run thing, four votes for the gnomes, four votes against. That left the casting vote in the hands of the chairman and he voted for the recommendation of the planning officers. Nan's gnomes would have to go and she was given thirty days to comply.

Katherine came back to The Spy that same evening to tell us what had happened.

"I'm very cross," she said, "in my view that decision had nothing to do with right and wrong but everything to do with a petty tyrant angry because someone dared to challenge him."

From his regular seat by the fire on the far side of the room came the sonorous voice of Old Falstaff. "As the great bard said, *'Loathsome canker lives in sweetest bud'.*"

His fox terrier Moonshine lying at his feet endorsed this with a sharp bark.

Katherine looked rather bemused. She was not aware of Old Falstaff's habit of quoting Shakespeare at every opportunity.

"What did he say?" she asked.

Jessica sighed. "Sonnet 35," she said. "He does this all the time."

Katherine nodded. "Canker is about right," she said, "it's not a matter of right or wrong, it's all down to interpretation and Melvin refusing to accept he might be wrong."

"Is there any way we can appeal?" asked Sylvia.

"Yes, but it's complicated. And time isn't on your side. I suppose they might have a change of heart and reverse their decision, but I doubt that will happen."

"We could always make it happen," said Jessica. We all turned to her and recognised that look in her eye which said she had a plan.

Katherine didn't know any of us well but her natural instincts were good and we saw a slight grin pass across her face.

"Probably time I made myself scarce," she said. Then addressing Jessica directly said, "Good luck. If you need any help I'll meet you in any lonely place after dark to talk things through but I won't actually be there, if you see what I mean."

"I see exactly what you mean," said Jessica, "and thank you."

Once Katherine had beaten a diplomatic retreat we crowded round Jessica and asked her what she was planning. We knew she had a mind that made a corkscrew seem straight so we were optimistic.

Her first question was, "How many Grade II listed buildings do we have in the village?"

We did a few calculations and Rupert finally said, "I would think about twenty-five to thirty if you include a few historic farm buildings as well."

"Don't forget the church," said Bev the Rev, "That's Grade I listed of course, but still counts."

"Good," said Jessica, "Now then, does anyone know where we can find Nan Mildew's grandson?"

"Not off hand," said Nigel, "but I can easily find out."

"You do that," said Jessica and proceeded to tell us what she had in mind. It was brilliant.

A few days later Jessica and Nigel went to visit Nan's grandson. I went with them – I love a good conspiracy. I was rather hoping that the gnome-building grandson might be called Gimli or Grumpy but it turned out his real name was Fred.

He made us coffee and showed us his workshop. It was fascinating – workbenches, piles of clay, pots and pots of paint. We sat on a wooden bench and Jessica outlined the problem that Nan was facing and he nodded.

"Yup, Gran told me all about that. Right miffed, she is. Load of old cobblers, if you ask me, but how can I help?"

When Jessica told him what she wanted his eyebrows vanished into his hairline.

"Wow, that's brilliant. Unfortunately I couldn't possibly

find that many from my own stock …"

Jessica's face fell but Fred went straight on, "… but I'll have a word with some of the others."

"Others?"

"Oh, yes, there's a huge gnome building fraternity in this part of the country. We all know each other and meet up regularly. We call ourselves the 'Three Foot High Club'.

I caught Nigel's eye and we quickly looked away. Jessica however ploughed straight on.

"So you think it's possible?"

"Oh, sure. Be nice if you could name the makers to anyone who asks. Always good for a spot of publicity. You'll have to arrange to collect them of course. I can give you all the addresses."

So we hired a couple of transit vans and working in pairs we toured round the various small potteries in a fifty mile radius of our own village, collecting gnomes of all sizes, shapes and postures as we went. Then came the job of distributing them which Rupert organised with his usual efficiency.

At last we were ready and Jessica moved on to the next stage of her campaign. She contacted our regional newspaper and as many of the local papers that she could. She also got in touch with one of the big London based dailies – best not to name it – but it was one of those which was always quite happy to print a dramatic story without fussing too much about the truth.

And so the headlines started appearing.

Local Council Victimises Old Woman

Old Lady, Gnome Alone, Victim of Council Spite

Gnome Sweet Gnome, but not for Mrs Nan Mildew

Katherine, fully briefed by Jessica, then stood up in a council meeting and asked why Melvin Turtlebong was singling out one of her constituents, Nan Mildew, forcing her to give up her beloved gnomes when others were allowed to get away with it.

"Always assuming that there is anything to get away with," she said, "Personally, I do not believe the gnomes contravene listed building regulations in any way."

Melvin Turtlebong was furious. "I am not singling out anyone," he shouted, "Those gnomes are against planning regulations that's why the council is acting."

"What about all the others then?" asked Katherine. "You haven't threatened them at all."

"What others."

Katherine sighed. "You really should do your research before having a tantrum," she said. "There are 29 Grade II listed buildings in that village, plus the church which is Grade I. Every single one of those properties has at least six gnomes in their front gardens and yet you've ignored those."

"That's because they're not there," yelled Melvin Turtlebong.

"Oh, yes, they are. Why not come and see?"

The Senior Planning Officer went white and put his head in his hands. The Chairman of the Council, glanced at him, sensed the Council was on a losing wicket, and popped in his two penn'orth. "If Councillor Warburton is correct then perhaps the Council should reconsider. Mister Turtlebong, may I suggest that you and Councillor Warburton visit the village and get an accurate idea of the gnome population?"

And so they did, accompanied by a group of reporters and photographers all tipped off by Jessica. Of course what they found was that outside every Grade II listed building was a collection of gnomes in a variety of sizes, colours and attitudes. There was even a gnome with the traditional fishing rod outside the church porch.

"Symbolic of Christ's *'fishers of men'*," said Bev the Rev with a straight face.

The press, both local and national, had a field day and the conclusion was inevitable. A re-convened meeting of the District Council Planning Committee was forced to accept that gnomes outside listed buildings did not contravene the regulations.

Nan kept her gnomes, adding another one from time to time. All the rest went back to the various potteries who had loaned them to us.

We held a celebration in The Spy to which Katherine Warburton came and bought the first round.

"To Jessica," she said raising her glass, "master planner and conspirator."

"And to the gnomes," added Harry, "and, as it happens, I've got one with me. I had it specially commissioned from Nan Mildew's grandson."

He opened the bag at his feet and produced a brightly coloured gnome with a huge grin on its face. The logo of our District Council was displayed on the front of his waistcoat but it was the unmistakable two-fingered gesture that the gnome was making which caught our attention.

That gnome now sits proudly on a shelf behind the bar in The Spy.

The Cuddly Companions' Cowboy Clambake

Nothing much ever happens in my Village in the Valley. We drift along peacefully, working, relaxing, chatting to our neighbours in pub or shop, feeding each other's chickens when someone goes on holiday and generally all rubbing along together with only a few minor rough edges. However just occasionally, the rough edges explode.

One of the most famous disputes in the village concerned a vintage Massey Ferguson tractor, an escaped eagle owl and a lady called Susie Mottram, a midwife from just over the county border. That one split the village in two and the final outcome was so shocking that by common consent no-one ever talks about it.

On the other hand the Cuddly Companions' Cowboy Clambake was widely discussed and, like so many other events in my Village in the Valley, passed into local folklore. Of course, at the beginning it didn't have anything to do with cuddly creatures, cowboys or clambakes. Exotic events like this don't come into being ready formed.

The Genesis, if you'll forgive the pun, came from Bev the Rev, our local curate. Bev the Rev is much loved in the village, more so than the vicar of our benefice, Victor Coggles who is not a popular man. We all expect – and hope - he will soon achieve his ambition of becoming a bishop as his natural instinct is to move along a diagonal. Nothing about him is straightforward.

However, who needs a power hungry vicar when you have a deeply caring curate and it was this deeply caring curate who unexpectedly appeared in The Spy one evening in March.

On this particular evening there was a group of us gathered by the bar and we all glanced up as Bev the Rev came in.

"Evening, Vicar," said Rupert and grinned as she wagged a finger at him.

"I am not a vicar, Rupert, as you very well know."

"More's the pity," muttered Nigel.

Harry stepped into the breach. "Well, regardless of your current standing in the hierarchy of the church, what can we get you to drink?"

Bev the Rev glanced round the assembled company. "Well, actually I was hoping to have a bit of a discussion."

"Who with?" asked Sylvia.

Bev the Rev paused for a moment and then said, "Well, I think, perhaps, all of you."

We looked at each other. This we were not expecting.

"Is something the matter?" asked Bill.

"No, not really." She hesitated. "Look, the thing is I want to organise a special function in the village. I tried to interest the Vicar but he thought it was a waste of time."

We all waited. There had to be more to it than this.

"I approached the Parish Council but they seemed rather preoccupied with financial budgets and arguments about planning permission. Then I tried the village hall committee but they said their priority this year was fund raising to install a new kitchen and they couldn't spare any resources for an event which wouldn't earn any income."

Jessica, as usual, cut straight to the point. "What sort of event are we talking about?"

"Something for children and families. Things are so difficult at the moment that it's hard for some families to even cover the day-to-day expenses. There's rarely anything left over just to have fun."

Several heads nodded. We all knew this was true. Our village is a very small village but even so we have at least six families who are kept from the brink by the local food bank.

"With you so far," said Harry, "but what brings you here?"

"You guys," said Bev the Rev simply. She glanced round at us. "Don't think I haven't noticed. You're the movers and shakers in this village. You get things done."

We looked at each other. We'd never thought of it like that but it was probably true. Those of us who gathered together regularly in The Spy were a mixed bunch. Some had been born in the village, some had lived here for ages and some were relative newcomers. However, the thing we all had in common was that none of us could abide red tape and if something needed doing, we just got on and did it. The occasion of the footbridge over the river to give better access to the village hall was a case in point but that's another story.

Bill made the next move. He had left the village in his teens to join the army, eventually retiring with the rank of Colonel in the Royal Engineers and is our resident strategic thinker.

"This will take a bit of planning," he said, "let's get another round in and go and sit down. What will you have, non-vicar?"

"A single malt, please," said Bev the Rev.

We settled ourselves round a table and Harry turned to Bev. "Right then, did you have anything particular in mind?"

Bev the Rev sipped her malt. "Well, not really. I did wonder about a picnic but that seemed a bit tame."

"Needs to be bigger than that," said Sunita, "if we're going to give families something to remember."

"How about a trip to a circus or a funfair or the zoo?"

"I'd prefer an event in the village. A kind of celebration of who we are as a community."

We nodded. We could see the sense in that.

Suddenly Jessica snapped her fingers. "Got it. We'll have a Summer Spectacular. Picnic, cakes, bouncy castle, face painting …"

"Yes, and a music group of some kind, games and activities …"

Bev the Rev thumped the table. "Brilliant, but does it need some kind of focus?"

"Yes," said Sylvia, "it does. Let me think" We waited while she took a sip of wine then she went on. "I know, how about we ask children to bring their favourite cuddly toys. Teddy bears, knitted dogs or bunnies, dinosaurs, owls whatever."

"Yes," said Nigel, "and we could extend it to the parents. Get them to bring a cuddly toy as well, either one of their own that they've still got or something they've borrowed."

Rupert grinned. "I like the sound of that. Be interesting to see what comes out of the woodwork. But I agree, we should certainly provide something for the parents as well. Make it truly a family occasion."

"I knew I was right to come to you guys," said Bev the Rev.

"Why wasn't the vicar interested?" asked Jessica, "I'd have thought something like this was a natural church event."

Harry snorted. "That man's a waste of space."

"Surplus in a surplice" muttered Nigel.

"I probably shouldn't say this," said Bev the Rev, "but you're right. The Reverend Coggles couldn't organise a Texas Clambake."

"A what?"

"Oh, it's an expression I picked up from American friends when I was working in the States a few years ago. I think the English equivalent would be '*Couldn't organise a piss-up in a brewery*'."

We were silent for a moment, contemplating the interesting life Bev the Rev must have had before coming to our village.

Sylvia was the first to recover. "Okay, we're making progress but now we need a name for this event."

"Something like 'The Summer Spectacular Village Picnic'," suggested Jessica.

"No. Needs something snappier." Rupert thought for a moment. "How about 'The Cuddly Companions Convention'?"

"Bit formal," said Harry, "but I like the 'Cuddly Companions' bit."

"Coming back to the parents," said Nigel, "what can we organise for them? A hog roast or something."

"We don't want anything where people have to spend money," said Bev the Rev, "that destroys the whole point."

There was silence for a moment as we all contemplated this requirement. Hog roast, bouncy castle, face painter, music group would all require some kind of fee and Bev the Rev was right. Money was tight and we did not want anyone excluded because of cost.

"I think I could persuade a face painter I know to do it for a good cause," said Sylvia.

"Ashley Fleming is part of some kind of band," said Rupert, "I daresay I could twist his arm."

"What sort of music do they play?" asked Nigel suspiciously.

"Folky stuff, I think," said Rupert vaguely. He paused for a moment. "Not sure they're very good actually, but maybe that's not really the point."

"I can play the ukulele," said Pawel.

"That'd be an interesting mix with Ashley," said Rupert, "but let's give it a go."

"Thanks, Pawel," said Bev the Rev, "But even after arm-twisting there'll still be some expenses won't there?"

We sighed. We knew this was true. There were always expenses.

Harry waved to Dan behind the bar and ordered another round. When our drinks had been replenished he lifted his glass in a kind of toast and said, "Leave the funding to me. I'll sort it."

Harry is a retired merchant banker and when he says he'll sort it, we know from experience that he will. We also know from experience it's best not to ask how.

"Right, that's settled," said Jessica, "now let's find a good name for it."

Bill suddenly started laughing. "I've got it," he said, "let's call it 'The Cuddly Companions Clambake."

"What?"

"It's perfect. Snappy and intriguing. Games and activities for the kids, barbecue for the adults. Bev said that the Vicar couldn't organise a Texas clambake, so let's show him that we can."

"What the hell is a clambake?" asked Nigel.

"Well technically a clambake is an outdoor party where they serve a bunch of seafood like lobster, shrimp, clams, and mussels. They're usually held on a beach."

We looked at each other.

"Where on earth would we source things like clams and mussels?" asked Jessica, "and would the kids want them even if we did?"

Bill waved an airy finger. "We don't need to be too literal about this. We could bung in a few grilled mackerel if you like but basically it would be the usual sausages and burgers. No one's going to quibble about the definition, are they?"

"And the beach bit?" asked Nigel, "I presume we're thinking of holding this on Roger's field down by the river. Not a lot of beach there."

"We're getting too bogged down in details," said Bill, "I went to a lot clambakes while I was in the States. There isn't a pure version, you can adjust it to fit the occasion."

"Well, I think it's a great idea," said Harry, "and it will be easy to promote. We shouldn't let a few details spoil a good title."

"Well, if we're serious about this, "said Jessica, "why not extend the idea and invite everyone to come wearing cowboy hats."

"Cowboys clutching cuddly companions," said Bev the Rev, "I knew you lot would come up with the goods."

Old Falstaff, sitting as usual by the fire with his fox terrier, Moonshine, at his feet, gave us the final seal of approval.

> *"The time of life is short!*
> *To spend that shortness basely were too long."*

None of us were really tuned in to Old Falstaff's passion for Shakespeare so, as usual, we all looked at Jessica.

She sighed. "Hotspur in Henry IV Part One. Don't any of you have any culture?"

We all looked at each other.

"So what do we think?" asked Bill.

"Let's do it," said Bev the Rev. And so the Cuddly Companions' Cowboy Clambake was launched.

THE INITIAL PLANNING went quite smoothly. A date was agreed, Roger's field was booked, Jessica designed a poster for the village notice board and also wrote a piece for Spyglass, the village magazine. Every family in the village was sent a personal invitation, Ashley Fleming's band agreed to perform in return for drinks, the sound of Pawel's ukelele was heard all over the village as he practised, and Sylvia put an arm lock on her face painter contact.

As usual, once the plans were made known the village entered into the spirit of the occasion and also, as usual, went way beyond the original spirit.

The village barbecue set was unearthed from Old

Crested's workshop where it had been stored over winter and the rust was brushed off it. Old Crested describes himself as an inventor though we think of him more as a lateral thinker. His real name is Newton Flotman but he's been known as Old Crested ever since that distant day in the past when he had organised an armada of crested newts to defeat an unpopular planning application. He was an enthusiastic supporter of the cowboy theme and had to be argued out of organising a steer wrestling event. Apart from the obvious problems we didn't think it would do much for the local cows.

We did wonder about reactions from the Parish Council and the village hall both of which, in a manner of speaking, had been bypassed, but there was no problem. Marjorie Fawcett, Chairman of the Parish Council, was one of the first to come forward with offers of help.

"Makes a nice change from arguing with those plonkers from the District Council," she was heard to say. Hugo Framlingham, chairman of the village hall committee just nodded absently and said to let him know if we wanted to borrow any tables or chairs.

Emery Jacobs and Ronald Trigg offered to run a *Surplus Vegetable Give-Away* stall, making contributions from their respective allotments, while Sunita said she would make extra jars of her special chutney.

Silas Pring, the Blenkinsop's cowman, suggested a ploughing competition but there wasn't enough field for that so we turned that down.

Esme Fritter and Clara Evans rounded up all the cake makers in the village and promised to organise tea and soft drinks plus a *Guess The Weight of the Cake* competition.

Dan and Maureen, landlords of The Spy, agreed to organise the drinks, having come to some arrangement with Harry and his mysterious funding source.

Roger offered to run a campfire stories activity and when that was agreed – subject to the subject matter being approved – ordered a large Stetson hat online to get into character, an idea quickly picked up by others.

The day itself began with a low mist over the river but by mid-morning that had cleared away and preparations were well advanced. The bouncy castle arrived and, when inflated, took on the shape of a western cavalry fort. Giant games – Jenga, Connect-4, Noughts and Crosses – were all set out on the grass. A gazebo had been erected for the face painter, a set of small rostra had been borrowed from the church and set up for Asley Fleming's band. Rupert had provided a small generator as Ashley had made it clear that he was an electric guitar man, none of your acoustic twanging for him.

"Not the quietest generator in the world," said Rupert, "just hope it's not louder than the band."

After a brief attempt for Pawel's ukelele to join in with Ashley's guitar – which was interesting but unconvincing – it was agreed that they would perform separately, turn and turn about.

Philip and Samantha Bracebridge had been persuaded to manage the drinks tent and to make sure that no underage drinking went on and all over age drinking was kept under control. Old Crested had built a realistic looking wild west bar out of old packing cases. It looked great but when Philip tried the saloon bartender trick of sliding a drink along the bar, it hit a splinter and spilled over. The final touch was a sign above the bar saying *Silver Spur Saloon* which Old Crested had made using a large soldering iron on a plank of wood.

A small bonfire was built on the far side of the field, surrounded by hay bales, all ready for the campfire stories and singsong.

Towards the end of the morning Nathan and Norman, who worked on the Grant family farm, started erecting a set of hurdles on the far side of the field. Silas the cowman was with them.

"What are those for?" Sylvia asked.

"No idea," I said but at that moment our question was answered. The Grants themselves, Percy and Kate, arrived in their Land Rover towing a trailer with three alpacas in it.

"Thought these might add a bit of local colour," said Kate cheerily, "another touch of America so to speak."

"Wrong bit of America," muttered Jessica, "you're around four thousand miles adrift."

"Don't alpacas spit a lot?" asked Nigel.

"Only if you try and nick their food or approach a female when she's pregnant," said Percy. "This bunch'll be fine."

Dan and Maureen provided lunchtime sandwiches for all the helpers and we were all set to go by the publicised starting time of two o'clock.

And they came. Kids in pushchairs, kids on scooters, kids walking, running, jumping. All clutching teddies and owls and rabbits and dinosaurs. One or two had shapeless objects that looked as though they'd been run over a few times or had accidents in puddles but were clearly still loved. There was even a knitted hippopotamus wearing a Stetson and a chequered bandana.

The parents too had entered into the spirit of the thing. Most wore cowboy hats, some had gone the whole hog with blue jeans, slant-heeled cowboy boots, spurs and tooled belts with fancy buckles. Some of the women were wearing detailed buckskin jackets with fringes. They would have looked somewhat incongruous at the best of times but when they came with teddy bears and felt rabbits tucked into their belts the effect was decidedly unusual even for our village.

Jessica couldn't quite believe it. "Did they already have this stuff at the back of their wardrobe," she wondered.

Humphrey Snape, our village bell captain, arrived holding a model railway engine above his head.

"I'm Butch Cassidy," he kept saying, "I'm holding up a train."

It was a memorable afternoon. The children all had great fun and so did the parents, even though the adults were not allowed on the bouncy castle. The giant games were very popular, as was the face painting. The sight of a young child in full cowboy gear emerging from the face painter's gazebo fully made up as a cat, caused Nigel to do a double take.

"Reminds me of Cat Ballou," he said. We exchanged glances. So the rumour was right. Nigel did have a thing for Jane Fonda.

Marjorie Fawcett had her teenage granddaughter, Naomi, staying with her that weekend and they had both offered to help. Marjorie was roped in to join Esme and Clara on the cake stall while Naomi soon found she had a full time job roaming the field, collecting discarded or lost cuddly companions and reuniting them with their owners.

Roger's campfire stories went down very well though a few of parents struggled with the concept of *Goldilocks and the Three Buffalos*, *Thomas the Covered Wagon and Friends*, to say nothing of *Peppa Hog* and *Dick Whittington and his Cougar*.

Jessica was not impressed. "Turn again, Whittington, Lord Mayor of Denver doesn't really play, does it?"

"I was going to do *Little Red Riding Hood* with a coyote," said Roger, "but I'm visiting the States next month and I thought the mention of "*Red*" might cause the ghost of Senator McCarthy to shove me in front of the Un-American House Committee so I changed my mind."

Ashley Fleming's band was … well, original, though a bit thin on the ground. There was Ashley himself on rhythm guitar, Melanie on a tambourine as well as being the lead singer and Lanky Larry with a kazoo. When challenged Ashley pointed out that it was a Saturday afternoon and most of his band members were either playing football or watching it on the telly. Even so they made a spirited, if slightly unusual, attempt at *Home, Home On The Range* and *Four Wheels On My Wagon*, before reverting to barely recognisable Bob Dylan songs, none of which were really suited to tambourine and kazoo.

On the other hand Pawel's ukelele was a great hit and he managed to get several of the parents dancing jigs.

Bill and Bev the Rev were in charge of the barbecue but all morning they were a bit coy about what delicacies would be on offer. They erected a canvas screen round the barbecue and no one was allowed inside. From time to time one of them would emerge with a request.

"Would someone please chase up those bread rolls and find those plastic forks."

To be honest, we were all a bit nervous about what sort of sustenance might be on offer in Bill and Bev the Rev's version of a clambake, but we needn't have worried. In the event the barbecue was a great success. Basically it was burgers and sausages but the burgers had been carefully shaped to fit into open-hinged clam shells and the sausages, when cooked, were thinly sliced and served up inside mussel shells. Not only was this innovative and in line with the theme of the afternoon but it also meant fewer sausages were required.

Bread rolls and huge bowls of salad completed the line up and most people came back for seconds.

Originally we had considered having a competition for the best dressed cuddly companion but after some discussion we decided that finding a winner meant there would also be losers and that was not the outcome we wanted for this event.

Instead we organised a Cuddly Companion presentation. Nigel marshalled all the kids into a line holding their companions, then Robert and Matilda Blenkinsop from the Big House, walked along the line, spoke to each child individually, asked about their particular cuddly and then held it up so everyone could see.

Afterwards each child was given a tiny box of chocolates which Harry had acquired from somewhere. We knew better than to ask where from.

By five it was all over. A lot of happy families trailed away with some of the kids snapping empty clam shells at each other like rebellious false teeth. The alpacas, which had behaved impeccably, were trucked away, back to what they no doubt considered was a safer environment. Silas was sad to see them go.

"Made a nice change from cows," he said.

A few cuddly companions were rescued from the grass, dusted down and put to one side waiting for their owners to discover they were missing. Eventually they all found their way back home apart from one tiny stripy tiger who was left sitting on a gate post. He was rehomed with a family who collected Winnie the Pooh toys. They thought that their Tigger would look after him.

Dan and Maureen left to open the pub, though, as Dan said, he suspected there wouldn't be many people in the bar that evening. As far as the village went he was right. Once everything was sorted out most of us gathered round the campfire, drinks in hand and Nigel, who used to be a Scout Leader in another life, led us in campfire songs.

> *There were rats, rats, as big as alley cats,*
> *In the store, in the store.*
> *There were rats, rats, as big as alley cats,*
> *In the Quartermaster's store.*
> *My eyes are dim I cannot see*
> *I have not brought my specs with me.*

I thought it was a fitting end to the day but Jessica just sighed.

"I'm off home before they start on *"Ging Gang Goolee, Goolee, Goolee, Goolee Watcha,"* she said, "I'm glad it's been a success but this cowgirl's for her bed."

She disappeared across the darkening field and then we heard a muffled curse. She had obviously discovered one of the parting gifts left by the alpacas.

One Bong Short of the Hour

My Village in the Valley is, on the surface at least, a quiet little place. A casual observer might think we would make an ideal location for one of these mythical England murder mysteries – pub by the river, line of old cottages, small village shop, people on bicycles, the occasional horse – but appearances can be deceptive.

To the best of my knowledge we have never had a murder here though to be fair some people still mutter darkly about what happened to Josiah Boggleberry back in the early days of the 20th century. As no one in the village today was actually alive then it would be difficult to come to the truth of the matter even if anyone was interested enough to try.

Josiah certainly did exist, his name appears in the parish records, but whether he was deliberately drowned in our river or fell in and couldn't get out or even, for that matter, whether he was drowned at all, none of us will ever know. Sufficient to say that Josiah has gone down in village legend as "that there man what was murdered in our river."

What is not in doubt is that when Josiah was alive he was a churchwarden in our parish church and one of his responsibilities was the maintenance of the church clock. Our clock is a large pendulum clock run by hanging weights, a truly historic timepiece. Back in the day Josiah had to climb to the top of the tower every six days to reset the weights to keep the clock running. Why every six days was a mystery known only to the clock maker. Also, if the clock got too fast or too slow, which could happen as these clocks were adversely affected by temperature and atmospheric conditions, he also had to lengthen or shorten the pendulum to bring it back on course. Quite an onerous job but because Josiah died – or was possibly murdered – in the early 1900s he was spared the additional task of having to physically change the clocks twice every year when British Summer Time was first established in 1916.

The clock winding duties passed from hand to hand over the years but eventually it became impossible to persuade someone to volunteer to climb the ladder every week, so sometime in the 1970s the winding mechanism was converted to have an electrical supply. This was fine, up to a point, but of course no electric motor could be set to make the necessary adjustments for BST and GMT. That still had to be done by hand.

And that was the crux of the current problem. The average age of the members of the Parochial Church Council is … well, let's just say that they've had to build a special rack for walking sticks inside the church porch. Nothing wrong with that, except when it comes to climbing up the bell tower of the church to move the hands of the clock forwards or backwards then none of the current members are really up for a steep flight of stairs, a spiral staircase and then finally a ladder.

Of course, it would be possible to find a handyman to do

this for them but that would need organising and somehow that never seemed to happen. The end result is that usually throughout the summer the church clock is one bong in arrears, chiming eleven instead of twelve and so on. By the time this has been acknowledged and someone has begun to think about doing something about it, it is nearly time to turn the clocks back again, so they just let it go.

Our vicar, the Reverend Victor Coggles, rarely comes to our church since he lost his battle with the PCC over the form of service, so he would never notice. Our curate Bev the Rev notices but she is very laid back. As she says, "Most people have a mobile phone these days if they want to know the time and anyway at least the clock is correct for six months or so."

It's probably fair to say that Bev the Rev sees the church clock as part of the historical fabric of the church, mainly preserved for traditional, decorative and artistic reasons, rather than a device to tell the time. Her exact words were, "A church tower without clock would be like a ballet dancer without a tutu."

The church in our village is quite an attractive building in a medieval sort of way. Its proper name is St. Jerome's of Antioch, but most people just call it St. Jerry's. There are plenty of similar churches all over our county which local people take for granted but which call forth many an "oo" and "ah" from visitors, especially those from abroad.

Marjorie Fawcett, chairman of our Parish Council, still tells the story of the time when a distinguished American doctor from California was visiting friends in the area and asked to see round the church. Marjorie was happy to take him but asked Matt Cookham, one of the current church-wardens, to give him the proper tour. The American was very impressed. When the stained glass windows had been admired, the ancient font reverently touched and a nice little contribution dropped in the collection box, they all stood outside and gazed up at the tower.

"Quite a place," said the American, "we don't have anything like this back home."

Matt had never been to California, all he knew about it came from watching western movies, so he just nodded wisely.

The American stretched out a hand and felt the rough stone at the base of the tower.

"Say, how old is this building?"

Matt thought for a moment. "Well," he said, "to the best of my knowledge that tower was started sometime in the twelve hundreds."

"Wow. That's pretty old," said the American.

"Of course," said Matt, "the porch there, that's a modern extension. They only built that in the 16th century."

The American clearly had trouble coming to terms with 'modern' and '16th century' being linked together.

The next, inevitable, question was why our church is called after Saint Jerome. No one really knows the answer to this so Matt gave the standard reply that the village has developed over the years.

"Well, it's like this. Back in the day, 300 and something AD to be precise, Jerome of Antioch translated the Bible into Latin."

"He translated it from Hebrew into Latin?"

"Yeah, Hebrew, bits of Greek too, I'm told. That's why we stick to the old form of service here."

The American's brow furrowed. "You mean, you still conduct services in Latin?"

"Don't be daft. No one round here speaks Latin. Foreign, innit?"

The services in our village church may not be in Latin but they are conducted along traditional lines based on the old book of Common Prayer. The PCC's determination to stick to this form of service caused some controversy with our Vicar, the Reverend Coggles, a few years ago. He wanted to change the service to the Common Worship version but the PCC were having none of it. It's true our regular congregation is quite elderly but whether they wanted to stick with the familiar form of service they were all used to, or whether it was just natural instinct to oppose any suggestion from the Reverend Coggles or whether it was just simple inertia, is hard to know.

Of course, inertia is a very compelling force and it was definitely inertia that kept the church clock one bong short of an hour for around six months of the year. A minor problem in the overall scheme of things until the night of the great storm.

That was certainly a night to remember. Some while back the Meteorological Office had started giving names to severe storms, presumably because it is difficult to be frightened of something which may be named after your favourite aunty.

In this instance that plan failed. Of course, whoever decided to name this storm Brünnhilde was probably not a fan of Wagner. Trying to allay people's fears by naming a storm after one of the Valkyries wasn't the smartest bit of thinking either, though in this case it turned out to be singularly appropriate.

Brünnhilde came roaring across the Atlantic – watching the images on television you could almost imagine her in a fiery chariot whipping her white horses on to greater effort. She smashed into Northern Ireland, bounced on to Liverpool, then rampaged right across England causing widespread floods and destruction over the countryside. By the time she hit our village she was really into her stride.

Within minutes of her arrival a large horse chestnut tree had crashed down across the bridge over the river, the roof of a storage shed at the village hall was lifted off the building and carried away, several cars had dents in their roofs as chimney pots were sent flying and landed in inconvenient places.

Luckily very few homes were seriously damaged, though there was quite a bit of repair work needed in gardens by the time Brünnhilde left us behind and headed for Germany.

"On her way home then," muttered Jessica.

However, while Brünnhilde herself caused the most obvious damage it was the attendant downpour of rain that really made itself felt. Several promising crops on the allotments were washed away, some of the footpaths became mud baths and the wind drove the rain into the top of the church tower with a result that only became apparent later. The river rose so high that even the car park at The Spy with its comprehensive flood barriers came under threat and for the first time since they were installed Dan took the precaution of erecting the flood gates across the pub doors.

The fabric of the church and its tower remained unscathed

throughout the ravages of Brünnhilde. Admittedly, it is a very solid construction and over the course of the last 800 years must have resisted quite a bit of weather, however, Nan Mildew, one of the most ardent churchgoers in the village, was convinced that the church had never been in danger.

"I'm given to understand that this Brünnhilde is some kind of pagan," she announced, "so it's not surprising that God wouldn't let her touch the church."

There's never any point in arguing with Nan, you might just as well try to build an igloo factory in the Sahara, so we just nodded and smiled.

However, as it turned out, the church did not escape totally. It was a few days later when a group of us were sitting in The Spy that we suddenly heard the church clock striking. That was not unusual. You could hear the clock very clearly in the main bar but as it only ever struck the hour, not the quarters, it had never been a problem.

It wasn't an auditory problem now either, but Harry suddenly said, "How many chimes was that?"

"Four, I think," said Nigel and then he suddenly realised. "But it's not 4 o'clock."

"No," said Harry, "It's not four o'clock, it's not any o'clock. It's twenty to eight."

There was silence as we all thought about that and then the clock majestically chimed again and we counted ten.

"That doesn't sound quite right," said Sylvia with masterly understatement.

Rupert sighed. "I suspect water's got into the mechanisms again," he said, "happened once before after a big storm and it was a bugger to sort out."

There was a brief lull then the clock chimed again, three bongs this time.

"Not going to be much peace in the village if it goes on doing that," said Dan from behind the bar.

But it did go on doing that. Once or twice every hour there would be a random series of bongs, amusing at first but it rapidly became irritating. Emery Jacobs, ever the opportunist, opened a book – you paid your ten pence and guessed how many bongs there would be in the next chime. Winner takes all, but even that palled after a couple of days.

Pressure was put on the PCC to get it sorted but they pleaded old age and no money so nothing was done and the bongs went on.

It was Dan who finally came up with a solution which he announced to us in the bar one night.

"My grandson Logan says we need to computerise the clock," he said, "then it can be controlled from the ground and will automatically reset itself for Summer Time and so on."

"Sounds good," said Bill. Bill is retired from the Royal Engineers and is always interested in anything technical. "What exactly does he suggest?"

"Well," said Dan doubtfully, "I think what he said was we needed a double flanged, perspective rambolt with floggles linked to the internet and operated by a laptop."

"Do what?"

"Well something like that anyway. Frankly I couldn't understand a word he was saying."

"But he reckons it can be done?" asked Bill.

"Oh, yes. When I outlined the problem he looked at

me and gave one of those deep sighs, as kids do when the stupidity of adults is beyond them."

"I think I'd better have a word with him," said Bill. "When's he coming up here again?"

"I could ask him to come this weekend."

"Then you do that. Time we got this clock business sorted."

Inevitably it was Nigel who put his finger on the ongoing problem. "Computerized gubbins or no, someone has still got to go up to the top of the tower to install it."

There was silence. None of us fancied the ladder at the top of the tower.

Finally Bill said, "I'll do it. It can't be any more dangerous than shoving a Bailey Bridge across a crocodile infested river."

As that wasn't something any of us had ever thought of doing we took his word for it.

Anyway that weekend Bill and Logan went into a huddle but it soon became clear that while Logan could offer a theoretical solution he had to do what he called *'a site inspection'* before he could come up with a specific plan.

"I'll just zip up there and have a look," he said, "then we can get this sorted out."

Dan, who was very fond of his grandson and very doubtful about the stability of the ladder, said, "No way, José."

Logan wanted to know who José was and why he was a spoilsport. Rupert stepped in quickly and said, "It's just a saying, Logan. The real problem is one of health and safety. The church's insurance doesn't allow 13 year olds to climb ladders on its premises."

Logan's look clearly said that he thought he was better

suited to climb a ladder than anyone else in the village but he was basically a courteous lad so he let it go. However, a visual inspection was clearly essential so Bill said he'd go up there and video the whole set up to show Logan what the mechanism looked like.

A small group of us went up the tower as far as the ladder to give Bill a hand. Or as Jessica put it, "to catch you when you fall." In fact when we saw the ladder we were glad it wasn't us going up it. It had definitely seen better days but Bill was undeterred.

"Better than the crocodiles," he said and up he went.

Mission accomplished we all settled down to watch the video. None of us had ever seen the inside of the top of the tower before so we watched with great interest.

Sylvia, who had been doing some online research into church clocks, told us that ours was a turret clock, the clocks that were originally built in high towers to strike bells to call the community to prayer.

Jessica, a confirmed atheist, muttered, "Well if it's going to go on striking about three times every hour there's going to be awful lot of praying."

"Traditional turret clocks are rare now," said Sylvia, "and even when they've been modernised to run by electricity you have to leave all the original workings untouched."

"Well, there's probably a preservation order on the winding mechanism now as well," said Bill, "from the look of it I'd say it was probably installed sometime around the time Alexander Graham Bell was inventing the telephone."

"But it was working more or less okay before Brünnhilde," said Nigel, "so what's changed?"

"Hard to say," said Bill, "my best guess is that none of the electrics meet modern standards. Probably a short somewhere."

Pawel nodded wisely. "We know this back in my home village in Poland. The clock on our church goes winky from time to time, especially after rain."

"I think you mean 'wonky'" said Jessica.

"Winky, wonky, no matter. When this happens the old folk say that God is angry with the town."

There was a moments silence.

"I think we'll stick with the faulty electrics," said Bill, "The pendulum seems to be working okay so I think it's the striking mechanism that's gone AWOL."

Bill sent a copy of the video to Logan by email and on his next visit they were able to have a more detailed conversation.

We gathered, from various comments made by Bill, and later Dan after Logan had gone home, that Logan had been less than impressed by the church as a building. As a child of the 21st century he could not understand how any public building would not have an integrated data network system as a matter of course.

Bill tried to point out that the skill of thirteenth century masons did not run to integrated network systems but Logan was not convinced.

He was even more outraged when he discovered there was no reliable power outlet at the top of the tower, just a simple mouse-chewed cable to an antiquated electrical motor which probably ought to be disconnected before it caused more harm.

"How did the guys who built this place plug in their

inspection lamps and battery chargers?"

By now Bill had come to the conclusion that some teenagers, Logan for example, were extremely bright in certain areas but although that brightness might have depth, it was definitely short of breadth. He decided it wasn't worth trying to explain so he suggested that they used a solar cell to power the electronic device. That made complete sense to Logan so another item was added to the shopping list.

In layman's terms we gathered that Logan's plan was to bypass the pendulum and install an electronic device in the tower to control the clock hands and the chimes. The pendulum and weights would be left in place but the electronics would have an internet link so that the whole thing could be controlled from below using a laptop computer.

There is no such thing as a secret in my Village in the Valley and the plans to change the church clock from a mechanical to an electronic system were soon widely known. Most people didn't really care so long as the random bongs stopped but inevitably there were objections. There will always be objections. Most of those complaining never went near the church at all except perhaps for Christmas, Easter and the occasional funeral, but that did not stop them and, of course, logic played no part.

"This is an outrage. if God had intended his clock to be run by a computer he would never have given us the typewriter."

"If you insist on putting a computer in a 13th century tower then it should be a 13th century computer."

"Installing modern electricity in an historic monument will bring a lightning strike down upon the church."

"And probably a plague of locusts as well," muttered Bill when he heard the last one.

The PCC had, of course, been involved in these discussions from the very beginning. They also had mixed feelings about "mucking about with history", as one person put it, but at the same time they realised the random bong problem had to be solved and anything that made their life easier was probably worth doing.

At some stage Old Crested – in his role as our eccentric village inventor – became involved as the electronic control system that Logan proposed to build had to be housed in something. The actual components occupied a very small space, but they needed to be enclosed in a structure that was weather proof in case any of Brünnhilde's relatives decided to come calling. When they first met, Logan and Old Crested got on like a house on fire, each recognising their respective creative skills separated only by sixty years.

At last everything was ready and Logan joined us in the bar – lemonade only – to demonstrate how it all worked. He linked his electronic device to the clock above the bar and, using the laptop, showed us how he could make the hands move and the clock strike. It was very odd hearing a small wall clock sound as sonorous as the clock in a church tower.

"How d'you do that?" asked Dan, "that clock doesn't have a striking mechanism."

"Doesn't need it, Grandad," said Logan, "there's a whole library of sounds on the laptop. You can select anything you like."

He clicked the mouse a couple of times and suddenly the clock above the bar struck three and then played the theme from Eastenders.

"Best not use that," muttered Jessica, "or we'll have a copyright problem."

Sylvia suddenly sat bolt upright. "Can it play any tune?" she asked.

"Sure," said Logan, "so long as the digital file is in the computer library."

"Right then," said Sylvia, "how about this? Suppose we added *Happy Birthday To You* to the computer library, then people could pay the church a small fee to have it played after the midday chimes on their birthday. People would love that and the PCC would make a bit of cash."

"Brilliant," said Harry, "and we could add other special occasions as well, such as Handel's firework music on November 5th …"

"Or some kind of ghostly music for Hallowe'en."

"In an English Country Garden for Midsummer's Day."

Yet again it was Nigel who identified the potential problem.

"That's all very well but do we really think that any member of the PCC could re-program a laptop computer to play music like this."

For a moment the excitement vanished, then Bill sighed. "It won't be a problem," he said, "the PCC have already asked me to manage the computer side of things. I don't think any of them even know how to turn the thing on."

It was clear that Sylvia's idea was very appealing and when it was explained to the PCC they also approved. Anything that provided another income stream, however small, was welcome.

So the next stage was to install the system in the church tower. Logan made one final appeal to go up the tower himself and oversee the installation but the answer was still "No." However, he did insist on going over the whole procedure in detail with Bill who listened patiently.

The next day Bill went back up the rickety ladder, "defying the crocodiles" as Jessica put it, and installed the device, constantly guided by Logan on a video link through his mobile phone. In fact the whole process went very smoothly, the only tricky bit was finding a suitable place for the solar cell to keep the main battery recharged.

Back on the ground Bill tested the system and it worked like a dream so everyone was happy. So happy, in fact, that it was decided to hold an official chiming opening ceremony. We all gathered in the churchyard just before midday. Dan provided snacks from the pub, Harry acquired some pseudo champagne from somewhere – we don't ask questions. Finally Bev the Rev was prevailed on to make a speech.

At five minutes to the hour she stood at the top of the church steps and said, "Friends and neighbours. I give you our new church clock chimes which will always bong properly in the future."

As she finished the clock began to strike but then, as the final stroke of twelve died away we were treated to a rousing reprise of the *Ride of the Valkyries*.

"A tribute to Brünnhilde," said Bill, "and may she never trouble us again."

THE PASSION OF AMBITION

A casual visitor to my Village in the Valley could be forgiven for thinking it is a gentle and quiet little country backwater. Well, yes, for much of the time it is, but occasionally, as in any small community, something unexpected suddenly erupts.

The epicentre of any village drama is usually The Spy. A group of us were in there one evening when suddenly the pub door was flung open violently and Philip Bracebridge appeared.

"Gently does it," said Dan, "have some respect for my door."

For many of us Philip's appearance and Dan's response was a case of déjà vu. Only too well did we remember the last time Philip had burst through that door bearing a tale of woe about the proposed nuptials of his daughter, Prunella. Philip doesn't come into The Spy very often so we assumed another crisis had erupted in his life, an assumption borne out by his opening words

"I need a drink," he said.

Dan had already reached for the whisky bottle.

"I'll get this," said Nigel, nodding to Harry. "You did it last time."

"I remember," said Harry, "best make it a double, Dan."

"Thanks," said Philip as he sank down onto a bar stool, a picture of dejection.

"Get that down you," said Nigel, "then tell us what's happened. This time," he added under his breath.

Philip took a long drink and then said, "It's my daughter, Prunella."

"Of course it's bloody Prunella," muttered Sylvia, "it's always Prunella."

Privately we agreed with her. Prunella was, what you could only describe as a determined young woman with a personality the size of a planet. At the age of sixteen she had played in her school's rugby team, 14 fellas and Prunella. This was a first for that school, but there was nothing in the rules that said all the team had to be boys, so the game went ahead and the spectators watched with a mix of emotions as Prunella mowed down the opposing forwards like an Arthurian knight scattering serfs right, left and centre.

As an adult that trend had continued. Prunella was, to put it mildly, difficult to resist. Last time Philip had burst into The Spy in a state of distress it had been to tell us the saga of Prunella's impending marriage. The problem back then had not been the marriage as such but the venue.

Prunella, being Prunella, had very strong views on the subject. With great rapidity she had moved through a variety of options all of which proved impracticable. A Buddhist ceremony, a chocolate-box church in Cornwall which only seated 40 people, a so-called *natural wedding* in a field, a Caribbean island and a three-mast schooner off the coast of the Isle of Wight.

Edwin, her fiancé, apparently had no say in the matter.

Eventually of course, they had to settle on the local registry office but not before Philip and his wife, Samantha, had been driven to despair.

Come the day Bill, Harry, Sylvia and myself all went to the ceremony mainly to support Philip. It was a disaster. There was a row over the room at the registry office which delayed proceedings beyond the legal time limit so Prunella and Edwin couldn't actually get married that day. The reception still went ahead but it was very much a DIY affair and in the middle of it we learned that Prunella had run off with Jason, the best man. Apparently he had promised her a fairytale wedding in a gypsy caravan in a highland glen in Scotland.

Since then the village had heard nothing of the perambulations of Prunella, but that situation was about to change.

The first drink had gone down without touching the sides so, at a gesture from Rupert, Dan poured Philip another. "What's she done now?" he asked.

"She's come home," said Philip miserably. Of course that's not the normal response from a father when his daughter returns to the family hearth but all of us in the bar that night understood his feelings.

There was a pause and then Sylvia tentatively asked, "And is … um … Jason … with her?"

Philip turned a mournful eye on her. "Oh, Jason didn't last," he said. "Apparently the gypsy caravan in the highland glen turned out to be too cold. Far as I can make out she only stayed three nights then moved into a house share in Fort William."

"So she didn't marry Jason?"

"Lord no ... silver linings and all that," he muttered to himself.

"Okay," said Nigel, "so what happened next?"

"Details are a bit vague," said Philip, "but as far as we can make out she moved south and went to work for a Lakeland sheep farmer. Healthy exercise, fresh air, all that stuff. We're not sure how long that lasted but we don't think long. She walked out on that, said the healthy exercise was all very well but not in constant rain. She also had a number of trenchant comments on the habits of sheep which I wouldn't want to repeat in mixed company."

I caught Jessica's eye and we both smothered a grin.

"You'll appreciate that news about her was sketchy," said Philip. "She was never very good about keeping in touch and to be honest we didn't like to ask."

"Not surprised," said Bill.

"However, the next we heard was that she'd joined a commune in Wales which was into self-sufficiency. A chance, and I quote, to get back to nature and be independent. As far as we can make out this was another brief passion that couldn't face reality. The commune may have been self-sufficient but it turned out that Prunella wasn't."

He paused and a brief grin crossed his face. "She rang up one day and said '*Honestly, Dad, you wouldn't believe the things they expect me to do*', and proceeded to give me a list. After she'd rung off I'm afraid I laughed. The idea of Prunella washing her smalls in a Welsh mountain stream and being expected to look after a crèche of small children before cooking a vegetarian meal over a campfire defies the imagination."

We considered this picture for a moment and agreed that '*defies the imagination*' was a good way to put it.

There was silence for a few moments. Dan poured out another whiskey and pushed it across the bar towards Philip who nodded his thanks.

Eventually the suspense got too much so Nigel said tentatively, "And then …?"

Philip sighed. "And then she moved on to somewhere in Cornwall, never did find out where. Got a job in a bookshop but that didn't last long. They sacked her because she kept telling customers that they'd get a better deal from Amazon."

There was another silence until Sylvia said, "And now she's come back to the village?"

"Yes. She was in Southampton for a few weeks but from the odd comment she's let drop I don't think her mother and I want to know what she was doing there."

"So what now? Do you think she wants a job at your place?"

Philip and Samantha live in our village but they manage a garden centre on the main road about five miles away.

Philip looked horrified at the suggestion. "God, I hope not. Business is up and down as it is."

And Prunella working there could complete the *down* we thought, but were too polite to say so.

"So what does she intend to do?"

"No idea, but Sam and I have been summoned to a meeting with her tomorrow evening and to be honest, I fear the worst."

As usual Philip insisted on buying a round of drinks

before Harry poured him into his car and drove him home.

As they went out the door we heard Old Falstaff, who was sitting on the other side of the room in his customary chair by the fire, mutter,

> *"How sharper than a serpent's tooth*
> *it is to have a thankless child."*

For once we didn't need Jessica to tell this that this was a quote from King Lear.

IT WAS SEVERAL WEEKS before we heard about the next development in the Prunella saga.

Philip came into the bar one evening, treating the door gently and looking resigned rather than desperate.

He waved away the offer of a drink. "No, you're all right, I'll just have a pint tonight, please, Dan."

We topped up our own glasses and clustered round, anxious to hear the next episode.

"So, is Prunella going to work at the garden centre?" asked Bill.

"Nothing that simple," said Philip. "When Sam and I arrived for our meeting as bidden Prunella announced that she wanted to start a women's rugby team in the village."

It's not often that the bar in The Spy goes completely silent but it did now.

"She wants to what …?" said Jessica.

"Start a village women's rugby team. You know she used to play rugger at school …" We all nodded. "And then she became a games teacher before all that … that … Edwin,

Jason stuff."

We nodded again. "Well, she says that women's rugby is the coming thing and the village should have its own team with her as the coach."

There was a pause and then Jessica said cautiously, "Well, I personally think starting a grassroots women's rugby team is a great idea, but in this village …?" She trailed off.

We knew exactly what was going through her mind. The suggestion was unquestionably admirable, but the total population of our village is not very large, and the number of women of possible rugby playing age is miniscule, so for this reason alone Prunella's plan was clearly a non-starter. Briefly, we considered the scenario of Vera Witheridge, who must be close on 80 if she's a day, leaving her walking frame on the touchline and running down the wing before passing the ball to Marjorie Fawcett, but even the most enthusiastic rugby fan among us couldn't make that work. It was a lovely image but then reality kicked back in.

After a moment Sylvia said tentatively, "And how's Prunella getting on?"

"She's not," said Philip, "no one's interested, well, of course they weren't, but I think Prunella was surprised by the hostile reaction. Apparently one woman she approached gave her a right flea in her ear. I think the exact quote was something like, '*With four kids and not enough money to feed them properly I have all the violence I need in my life, thank you very much.*'"

"So has she given up?" asked Nigel.

"I think she's about to," said Philip, "I know she's spoken to various people in some of the other villages around here but the result's the same."

"Hardly surprising," said Jessica, "it's all wonderfully impressive, and I admire her ambition but sorry, Philip, your daughter's potty."

"I know," said Philip gloomily, "but she's still my daughter."

The next thing that happened was that Prunella disappeared. According to the Bracebridges she went up to bed as usual one night but in the morning she was gone.

It was difficult to tell whether Philip and Samantha were worried or relieved. Maybe *'slightly concerned'* was the best way to put it. After all she was their daughter and they didn't know where she was, but on the other hand life was a lot less stressful when she wasn't around.

Bill, slightly mischievously, suggested we open a book for suggestions as to what she might be doing now but we turned that down on the grounds of bad taste. As it turned out none of us would have won anyway.

So that was that, or at least that was that until several months later when the circus came to town. That statement sounds much more exciting than the reality. This was no Billy Smart's or Bertram Mills Circus affair as used to happen in the 1950s and 60s. Several of the older people in the village could remember being taken to that kind of circus to see performing elephants, acrobats, lions and clowns.

The lions and elephants may be a thing of the past but as it happens we do have a travelling circus in our area of the country which pops up from time to time in the summer, touring around and setting up camp on playing fields or large village greens. It's called *Paddy's Pageant* though as

'*Paddy*' speaks with a broad East Anglian accent and '*pageant*' is as fine an example of hyperbole you'll ever find, modern circus organisations like *Barnum & Bailey* or the *Moscow State Circus* don't have much to worry about.

Even so *Paddy's Pageant* is very popular and is actually quite fun. It makes a change to sit on a wooden bench in a tent, eating popcorn and watching acrobats and tumblers, clowns and jugglers, trapeze artists and comedians, all with the flair and razzmatazz and music that is really very entertaining.

On this occasion they were performing in a seaside town about 20 miles away and a small group of us decided to treat ourselves to a day out. Bill offered to drive, so Harry, Sylvia, Jessica and I joined him in his 4x4 and we set off. Privately I thought that Bill drove as though he were still driving a jeep across enemy terrain but we got there safely. We started with a pub lunch in the *Mermaid and Porpoise* on the seafront. It was good, but we all agreed, not a patch on The Spy back home. Then we had a stroll along the prom in the sort of wind that is usually referred to as bracing but which I call cold, and then finally it was time to make our way out to the field where the circus had pitched its Big Top.

Grown ups we may be but there is something infectious about a fair or a circus that touches the inner child in all of us. Sylvia bought candy floss, the rest of us chose popcorn and we settled down on the wooden benches to have fun.

And it was fun. Young ladies in spangled tights doing things on a trapeze that left us gasping, clowns attempting – unsuccessfully – to juggle bottles of water while telling jokes we had first heard forty years ago. Why, I don't know, but in that atmosphere they were still funny.

A conjurer who was actually quite good at all the usual tricks, but my favourite bit was when he said, "Now then, ladies and gentlemen. Traditional conjurers often do the famous trick of sawing a lady in half. But tonight I'm going to reverse that trick so if two half ladies would like to step forward then we can commence the rejoining process."

Not the greatest joke in the world but it brought the house down. And so the show went on. Acrobats bending themselves into impossible shapes, musicians – some good, some of them clowns pretending to be good and in the middle of them all a traditional ring master in red coat and top hat holding it all together. It was indulgent, of course but we were really enjoying ourselves.

And then suddenly our whole day shifted gear. The Ringmaster announced, "Now, Ladies and Gentlemen, *Paddy's Pageant* proudly presents the wonderful, the marvellous, the unsurpassed Lady Samson, the strongest woman in the world."

The trumpets blew a fanfare and into the ring sprang this majestic female in tights and glitter who started by lifting the ringmaster off the ground and then proceeded to perform a series of feats of strength that had the audience gasping in amazement.

Four of us did our share of the gasping too but Jessica was silent. After a moment she said, "You do realise that's Prunella Bracebridge, don't you."

We didn't, and we hadn't, but Jessica was right. It was definitely Prunella.

On our way back to the car we had a brief discussion.

Do Philip and Samantha know what Prunella is doing and, if they don't, should we tell them or let sleeping Samsons lie? We decided to let them lie.

And that was that until several months later. We were gathered, as usual, in The Spy one evening when suddenly the pub door was flung open violently and Philip Bracebridge appeared.

"Gently does it," said Dan, "have some respect for my door."

This had become a recurring theme where Philip was concerned so we all looked at each other and wondered what had happened now.

"Large scotch, is it?" asked Nigel.

"No, no," said Philip, "well, yes, yes, actually but this round's on me. Fill up the glasses please, Dan."

When everyone in the pub had a full glass, including two strangers who had only popped in for a swift half, Philip took the stage.

"I want you all to join me in drinking a toast to my wonderful daughter, Prunella."

We dutifully raised our glasses but we were more than a little puzzled. The words *'wonderful'* and *'Prunella'* did not often go together when Philip was talking.

Jessica, who is to tact what ferro concrete is to hang gliding, said, "What's she done now, Philip?"

"Well," said Philip, "it's like this …"

We sighed inwardly. We had long since learned that Philip's stories always started at a tangent so we settled back to listen.

"You remember how Prunella vanished after her failure to

recruit a local women's rugby team …?"

Yes, we remembered.

"Well, we didn't know where she had gone for a long time but a few weeks ago we discovered she had been working as the Strong Woman in a circus, you know, that *Paddy's Pageant* thing that pops up round here from time to time."

There was a small murmur of amazement from the crowd in the bar while Harry, Bill, Jessica, Sylvia and I tried to avoid looking at each other.

"Bit of a surprise, to be honest," said Philip, "apparently she was billed as the unsurpassed Lady Samson, the strongest woman in the world." He gave a shy sort of smile. "Actually, Sam and I were quite proud of her, showed a lot of initiative, we thought."

I glanced at Sylvia and she glanced at me. We were clearly both thinking the same thing. Philip might have been proud at having a daughter known as Lady Samson, but we strongly suspected that Samantha's reaction would have been quite different.

"Anyway," Philip went on, "that's not the big news. She's not with the circus anymore."

"So what is she doing?" asked Nigel, "must be good to warrant drinks all round."

"Oh, it is, it is. You see what happened was that the circus was performing in a field up on the north coast somewhere. The show was over and the crowd was leaving when suddenly there was a cry of 'Fire' and they realised a barn in the next field was ablaze. Most of the circus people rushed across to see if they could help but the building was well alight. As they stood there the frantic farmer came running up yelling

'*My horses are in there and they can't get out.*' Well, I think the general feeling was that the horses had had it, but suddenly Prunella grabs a bucket of water, pours it over her head and heads for the burning barn."

Philip paused to take a drink. It seemed a good moment for a crowd reaction so we all said, "Ooo …"

"She must have been mad," said Philip, "the barn doors were fastened but she kicked them in, dived into the flames and led the horses out of the barn."

"Were the young lady badly hurt?" asked Emery Jacobs.

"Well, she was a bit burned," said Philip, "but by then the fire brigade had arrived and ambulance as well so they carted her off to hospital."

"And is she all right now?"

"Pretty much," said Philip, "but the big news is …"

At last, we all thought.

"… that when she came out of hospital she went down to London and applied to join the London Fire Brigade as a firefighter. They've accepted her and she starts her full training next week. So, let's all raise our glasses to my daughter, Prunella."

"Good for Prunella," said Dan, "next round's on the house."

We filled our glasses and lifted them to Prunella. We had always thought of her as a real pain in the neck but we had to acknowledge that she had come good in the end.

However, some of us did pause to wonder how long it would be before we had news of a champion London Fire Brigade Ladies Rugger Team.

You Have To Go With The Flow

A long forgotten poet once said:

> *A river runs gentle in front of our door,*
> *Its tinkling sound will lull you to sleep.*

One of the main attractions of my Village in the Valley is the river that flows through it. As rivers go it is not huge. In theory it is wide enough and deep enough to take a small motor launch, except the various bridges along the river are too low to allow anything bigger than a kayak or a rowing boat to get under them. That's fine by us, we get the beauty of the river without the mad boat owners you find on bigger rivers, the ones who think they're taking part in the Round Britain Powerboat Race.

Our village pub, The Spy, stands on the bank of the river with a terrace that attracts a lot of visitors on summer evenings. The other buildings in our main street are separated from the river by the road but at the far western end of the village, where the road begins to rise slightly, there are a number of houses whose gardens run down to the water's edge.

Many village events are held on one of the riparian meadows, but the river itself can also be the focus of activity.

One such example is the annual charity raft race. Each summer local groups are invited to construct a raft out of various odds and ends – usually involving oil drums, pallets, lots of rope and optimism - and then they race downstream from the bridge in the neighbouring village to the finishing post at our bridge.

The quality of the raft construction is variable and not every raft makes the journey intact. Bill is on the race organising committee and, having been in the Royal Engineers, he takes an active part, not just in the construction of a raft, but also as one of the paddlers. It has to be said that, amid the watery mayhem that the race generates, Bill's rafts have never been known to sink.

The whole thing is great fun and traditionally spectators line the route, squirting the paddlers with water pistols and cheering on their favourites. Most of the raft crews are in costume, some better suited to a ducking in the river than others. Over the years we have seen pirates (pretty obvious), Kings and Queens, Roundheads and Cavaliers, serving wenches and footmen, but no matter how creative the costume we have never had a raft race without at least two or three crews managing to sink or overturn before the finishing line.

Other water-based activities in our village include *Pooh Sticks* and *Duck Races*. Sunita Devi, who helps out with the *Toddlers Play Group* (known unofficially as the *Munchkin Mafia)*, is a keen supporter of *Pooh Sticks* and managed to recruit lots of players once she had read them the relevant *Winnie-the-Pooh* stories. Of course, this game only became practical once we had the footbridge linking the car park of

The Spy with the village hall on the other bank. Before the footbridge was installed there were a few attempts to play *Pooh Sticks* on the road bridge but, as that is very narrow, there was always the risk of a close encounter with a lorry so it never caught on.

Duck races are also popular, though they take place over a shorter distance than the raft race. This *Duckling Derby* was started some years ago by Dan and Maureen at The Spy, presumably to encourage people into the pub. Plastic ducks of all kinds take part, ducks with RAF insignia, ducks dressed up like American policemen or Henry VIII, ducks in dinner jackets, ducks with Christmas hats on and some which are simply duck ducks. They are all lovingly released at the same time from the bank in Roger's field about a hundred metres upstream from the Spy so they can drift along on the current. The winner is the person whose duck reaches the car park footbridge first. The prize is usually a bottle of wine or a box of chocolates depending on the age of the duck owner. It's a very popular event, and not just for the contest between competitive plastic Anseriformes. I know for certain that some serious off-course betting goes on amongst the older members of the village.

So you see, there is no doubt that, on or off the water, the river is an integral part of life in my Village in the Valley.

However, before we get too idyllic I should point out that the river is not always benign. After a prolonged bout of heavy rain the water level inevitably rises and in extreme circumstances the river can burst its banks. It is not unusual for the meadows along the riverside, both upstream and downstream of the village, to be flooded but that is partly their purpose – to act as a flood plain. Most of the houses in the village are high enough for flooding not to be a problem. The only building which is at risk is The Spy.

Years ago, shortly after I first moved back to the village, we had a very heavy storm and the ground floor of The Spy was completely flooded. A lot of damage was done so when the water eventually went down, Dan and Maureen decided that precautionary measures needed to be taken. That was when they constructed the outside terrace along their section of the riverbank. They made it high enough to stop casual flooding and also built a parapet which extended right round the car park. As a precaution Dan also installed flood gates which could rapidly be assembled across the doors into The Spy if the weather became excessive.

I remember well the *Flood Gate Party* we held after they had been installed. Dan reckoned that the more people in the village who knew how to erect them, the better it would be if help was ever needed in a hurry. In fact the process is quite simple. There are slots mounted on each side of each door into which a series of plates, which are kept in an outside shed, can easily be slotted into place. The plates are quite heavy so outside help is welcome which is why Dan and Maureen organised a demonstration party, boosted by free drinks and platefuls of Maureen's bacon butties. As far as I know the gates have only been erected once, the time when Storm Brünnhilde hit the village, and even then they weren't actually needed.

"Still, better safe than sorry," said Maureen.

We are fortunate that we don't get a lot of debris in the river. Clumps of foliage, the odd branch, very occasionally a plastic bag, but on the whole it is a very clean stretch of water. There was the time, about a year ago when on a very violent night a large tree trunk came floating down the river, presumably having been blown down in the storm. It rode the waters well, slid neatly under our footbridge but when it reached the narrow arch which carries the main village road over the river, the current turned it sideways and it jammed itself again the brickwork. The water began building up behind it and it was clear that the road itself might flood.

Dan rang Roger Fraser who was soon on the scene with some of his farm workers and one of their tractors. They all got very wet but it wasn't long before the tree trunk had been hauled out of the river and lay dripping in the car park of The Spy.

Roger offered to have it chopped up but Dan had a better idea. He had a word with Old Crested, who could turn his hand at anything practical. A week or so later, when the log had dried out a little, he came along with his chain saw and sculpted the tree trunk into the shape of an alligator with a set of extremely fearsome teeth and its back hollowed out to make a seat. Dan installed this on his terrace and it soon became a very popular photo opportunity, especially with the kids.

Although in my Village in the Valley we have the flood problem pretty much under control, flooding over much of the country has got steadily worse over the last few years. Farmers like Roger and Percy Grant have no doubt about one of the main causes for this.

"Concrete," says Percy, "stands to reason. More and more housing estates means more and more concrete foundations.

Completely buggers the natural drainage of the land."

"And these days a lot of people concrete over their front gardens to make parking spaces," added Roger. "That doesn't help."

Of course drainage is always an important part of water management. I remember when I was having a new patio laid behind my house the first thing the builder said was, "Where does the water flow?"

He investigated the slope of the land, the site of the existing drains and before laying the patio itself, he laid a pipe to carry away any excess water and dispose of it safely.

"A blocked drain you don't need," he said, "especially as you can't aways find where the blockage is."

It was some years later that Majorie Fawcett unintentionally proved the accuracy of that statement.

Marjorie Fawcett is the Chairman of our Parish Council and she is, what you might call, a no nonsense chairman – oh, and it's always 'chairman'.

"None of this 'Chair' nonsense," she is fond of saying, "I might look squat and square but I am not a piece of furniture."

She runs Parish Council meetings firmly but fairly. If a committee of any kind is to be effective there must always be an expression of different views to promote discussion. Without discussion there isn't really any point in having a committee at all, but discussion – which can also mean argument – can easily get out of hand. Allowing discussion, but not letting it get out of hand, is Marjorie's forte.

She has an attribute which is rare amongst committee members and non-existent in professional politicians. She listens to what people say. She is very good at allowing different views to be expressed then, sensing the overall feeling of the meeting, she proposes a solution. As her proposals tend to be a triumph of common sense over emotion they are usually accepted. Once accepted, that's that. Majorie is a very relaxed person, but once she has drawn her line in the sand she pours concrete into it and that's that.

Anyway, back to drainage. Marjorie lives in an old house on the western edge of the village. It is an interesting house. It was built in the 1870s and from the front it looks pretty normal, two storeys, central front door, windows either side. What isn't immediately apparent from the road is that there is a lower level. The house is built on the slope down to the river so it is a two storey house at the front and a three story house at the back. The lower level has two main rooms. The one at the front is a kind of scullery which Marjorie uses as an inside greenhouse, washing pots, storing tools and so on. The other, which has no natural light, is the utility room, housing washing machine, tumble dryer, freezer and her husband's collection of naval flags of the world which she didn't have the heart to dispose of after his passing.

It was in this room that the problem first appeared.

When she saw the puddle of water Marjorie's first thought was that she'd been careless getting stuff out of the washing machine. She mopped it up but when it reappeared she knew something was wrong. She checked the freezer in case that was faulty and was defrosting itself. No, the freezer was fine but the puddle persisted. No matter how much she mopped, the water kept coming and the problem was clearly getting worse.

She realised that this could not be ignored so she rustled up some help in the village and moved all the electrical appliances upstairs. It wasn't terribly convenient having the tumble dryer in the sitting room and the freezer in her bedroom but until the problem was solved there seemed no alternative.

The next stage was to contact her insurance company. As is the way with many insurance companies they weren't terribly keen on actually doing anything but Majorie is a forceful personality and they finally agreed to send an insurance assessor round to view the damage.

It was a fortnight before he actually turned up with Marjorie getting more tight-lipped by the day but when he did come he was less than helpful.

"Well, I can see your problem," he said which, as he was actually standing in about a quarter of an inch of water at the time, was not a particularly brilliant observation.

"I know what the problem is," said Marjorie, "what I want to know is what are you going to do about it?"

The man drew in his breath like a car mechanic viewing a faulty engine.

"Well, there's been a lot of rain recently," he said.

I know there's been a lot of rain," said Marjorie who by now was getting quite irritated. "We were hit by Storm Brunhilde a few months ago. It damaged the church clock, the fields were flooded and the river overflowed."

"Ah," said the insurance assessor, "that'll be it then. These properties by the river are always liable to flooding. There's an exclusion clause in your insurance contract about that."

"Oh, no, there isn't," said Marjorie, "I negotiated that

out of the spec when I insured this property with you. We may look out over the river but the slope down to it is very steep. We've had this argument before, there is a drop of over twenty feet between the ground floor of my house and the river. If this water had been caused by the river flooding then a national disaster would have been declared and the United Nations would be taking people out of here by helicopter."

The insurance assessor sniffed. "Maybe I should have a word with your husband," he said.

"Well, you can try," said Marjorie, "he's about a quarter of a mile down the road."

"Will he be home soon?"

"I doubt it. He's in the churchyard. He's been dead these last twelve years."

The insurance assessor was clearly not used to dealing with feisty old ladies. "Hmm. Well, I'll take a couple of pictures and you'll be hearing from us."

Marjorie was not impressed.

Another fortnight passed. The water level on the utility room floor increased to about half an inch, only prevented from flowing out of the room by the concrete step in the doorway. Majorie took a broom and bucket to it each day and poured the water away down the outside drain.

Finally she had a letter from the insurance company which caused her to utter a word that respectable elderly ladies are not expected to know.

In summary it said that the assessor had not been able to reach a firm conclusion but had agreed to authorise a builder to come and look at the problem. In due course a builder came, he also sniffed and did the indrawn breath noise so

Marjorie knew he wasn't going to be any help. Finally he announced his verdict.

"Act of God," he said, "Amount of rain could not be foreseen. It's caused a rise in the water table. Not an insurance problem. Pity you decided to build here."

"Decide to build here?" Marjorie said angrily. "This house was built in 1873. How old do you think I am?"

He sniffed again. "Never guess a woman's age," he said, "always leads to trouble."

Resisting the temptation to push his head under the water which was still rising she said, "Okay, Act of God. I'll take that up with God later but for now what can I do about it."

He shrugged. "Frankly, I think your only hope is to install a sump. You'll need to have this floor up, dig a deep hole in the middle, then dig a trench across the room, then across the floor in the next room, across your patio and across your lawn. I suggest you take the trench right down the garden for a hundred feet or so."

"Dig everything up? Floors, patio, lawn?"

"Don't see you have a choice. Once you've dug your trench you lay a pipe in it, fill in the trench and make good. Then the sump will trap the water and pipe it away from the house."

"That sounds like a huge undertaking."

"Yup. Give you a quote for it if you like."

"If you do the job will the insurance company pay for it?"

"Nah, not a hope. Act of—"

"— God yes, I got that. Well, in that case I'll get my own quote thank you."

"Suit yourself."

As so often in my Village in the Valley, Marjorie took her problem to the crowd gathered in The Spy. She was obviously very irritated so Dan poured her a large gin and tonic and we asked her to explain.

The first five minutes was a rant against insurance companies and opportunistic builders, but once her spleen had been truly vented, she gave us the facts.

"Well, it won't be hard to get the job done," said Nigel, "Is that something your firm could handle, Rupert?"

"Sure," said Rupert, "but it's not a skilled job. I reckon Matt Cookham here in the village could sort that out. He'd be cheaper too."

"Fine by me," said Marjorie, "if it's got to be done, then I'd rather have someone like Matt do it. Even so, it's not the doing that's the problem, it's the disruption and the damage it will cause."

"Sounds like a long job," said Jessica.

"And I think it will be a very messy one," added Pawel Adamski, "my father, he was a plumbing man and he always spoke badly about drains."

"That's not very reassuring, Pawl, but I suspect you're right. However, my point is – why? We've had heavy rain before, we've had floods before but I've never had puddles in my basement before."

There was silence as we contemplated the problem and Harry bought her another gin.

Bill, who'd been very silent through all this, suddenly said. "I've had a thought …"

We all turned to look at him. Bill is a practical man and his thoughts are usually worth taking seriously.

He turned to Marjorie. "Are you alright for a couple of days, Marjorie? I appreciate it's not very convenient but I have an idea. I just need to explore it further."

There was a pause and then Marjorie nodded. "Okay, Bill, but I really do need to get it sorted soon."

"Of course. Quite understand. Leave it with me."

A few days went by then Bill rang Marjorie. "Could I come round tomorrow? I've got someone who might be able to help."

He turned up the following morning with a young man with a long straggly beard who was carrying what looked like a small lawnmower with a computer screen on top.

"Morning, Marjorie," said Bill, "this is Liam."

"'Ow do," said Liam.

"Can you show us the basement room where the problem is," said Bill.

"Of course. Come in. I've emptied it once this morning so it'll be damp but not flooding yet."

They tramped down the stairs with Liam holding his machine protectively to his chest. When he saw the basement room his eyes lit up.

"Oh, boy," he said, "this is going to be fun."

Marjorie drew Bill to one side. "What is that thing?" she asked.

"Ground penetrating radar," said Bill. "Why don't we leave Liam to play and we'll go and have a coffee."

It was about half an hour later when they heard Liam call, "Got it, Bill. Come and look."

Marjorie and Bill went back downstairs to find a rather damp Liam grinning all over his face.

"You were right, mate. I've found it. Went over it several times to make sure. Once I was certain I marked it. See?"

Marjorie peered down at the floor to see an area about a metre square marked out in fluorescent yellow paint.

"Um, what exactly is it you've found," she asked.

"He's found your sump," said Bill. "If we get Matt to come in and dig there I think we can solve your problem with a minimum of fuss.

And so it proved. Matt arrived with a jack hammer and, watched by Bill, removed the segment of floor marked out by Liam's paint. He did not have to go very far down before he came across a vertical drainage pipe that was full of water.

"Aha," said Bill and got down on his hands and knees.

Probing deeper they found a horizontal pipe leading off the vertical one which was also full of water. Matt went away to fetch a set of drainage rods and then they prodded away at the horizontal pipe. It took a lot of rods but finally the blockage was free and the remaining water in the basement room drained away.

That night in The Spy Bill explained his train of thought.

"It was when Marjorie said it had never happened before," he said. "I thought, well, the house has been there since the 1870s and there's been lots of heavy rain over the years so why hasn't it happened before?"

Harry nodded. "Because the problem had been foreseen."

"Exactly. The Victorians weren't stupid builders. They knew if you built a house on a hillside overlooking a river then the water table would be bound to change from time to time, so they built in a drainage system to deal with it."

"Which over time got blocked up," said Nigel.

"I was pretty sure it must be there," said Bill, "so I got Liam in and his GPR found it."

"Well, I'm not buying you a drink on the strength of that, Bill," said Marjorie.

We all looked at her and she grinned. "No, I'll buy you a case of scotch. I think you're brilliant."

Two months later there was another violent storm and again our placid river became a torrent and burst its banks. However, Marjorie's basement room stayed dry thanks to the skill of Victorian builders and Bill's instincts.

Someone, we suspect Nigel but we're not sure, wrote a parody for our village magazine.

A river runs gentle in front of our door,
Its tinkling sound will lull you to sleep.
But when it gets angry it pours over the floor
The damage it causes will make you weep.

Who's A Pretty Boy Then?

There have always been certain incidents in my Village in the Valley which remain in the memory. Old Crested on an electric lawn mower destroying the combined armies of the Romans and the Iceni, Sholto and Lana Frobisher's attempt to build an air raid shelter, or the truncated Harvest Festival service which became known as *The Day of the Harvest Goat,* are just a few that come to mind.

Then there was the time when a bus got stuck on the bridge over the river, an event which led to the *Pets in Odd Poses* competition in our village magazine. Not an obvious connection you might think but that's my Village in the Valley.

What happened was this.

The road leading out of our village crosses the river on a very narrow single track bridge, only just wide enough for a lorry or a bus. On this occasion a motorcyclist tried to overtake the bus as it was approaching the bridge, accelerated across in front of it at the last minute and vanished up the road. The bus driver, seeing a potential accident unfolding in front of him, slammed on his brakes, the bus skidded on the wet surface, slid sideways and neatly jammed itself between the two bridge parapets. It could neither go forward nor back and nothing could get past it in either direction. Fortunately no one was hurt.

However, the squeal of brakes and the thud as the bus hit the parapet brought everyone within earshot out onto the street. Before long, due to the telepathic information system that exists in small villages, many more people arrived to join in the fun.

Of course, whether you think a bus wedged on a bridge – and so blocking the whole road – is fun, probably depends on your point of view. If you're a passenger on the bus whose journey has been interrupted then *fun* probably isn't the word that comes to mind, especially when you've had to walk carefully along the bridge parapet to the other side of the river and wait for a replacement bus.

Or if you are driving a car, lorry, whatever and you come across a bus well and truly wedged between the two parapets of the bridge and realise your only option is to do a 3-point turn and find a way round which will involve a five mile detour, then again *fun* is probably not your first thought.

Or, more extreme, if you are the driver of a lorry of ready mix cement and you're faced with a blocked bridge, where you can't turn round and your cement is rapidly hardening, of all the words you might use *fun* would not be one of them.

But for the rest of us, for whom the screech of brakes and general hubbub had dragged us away from DIY or the ironing or day time telly to come and see what was going on, it was – if not fun exactly – something more interesting than whatever it was that we'd been doing.

Of course we didn't just stand by, we helped where we could. We assisted people to edge their way along the bridge parapet to safety, we explained alternative routes to stranded drivers, we provided hot drinks for those who were a bit shaken. What we couldn't do was shift the bus. That took a couple of hours and a large tow truck, but even then the police would not reopen the bridge to traffic until it had been inspected by a structural engineer.

I've always found it interesting how quickly people gather at any kind of scene like this. Most people genuinely want to help if they can but the overheard conversations in the crowd can be very entertaining.

"Mummy, why is that bus trying to drive into the river?"

"No idea, darling. Now I'm just going to ring your father to remind him to collect Gran from the opticians because we both know he won't remember, will he?"

Or … "That's a funny place for a bus stop."

Though on this occasion my favourite one was … "I do hope he didn't hit the kingfisher …"

Once the immediate problems had been sorted out there wasn't really much to see but events like this always attract a good crowd so we all hung around for a while. At one stage I noticed that a large ginger cat had appeared and was perched on the bridge parapet apparently gazing intently into the bus driver's cab.

Then Doreen Fawcettt arrived with Bruno, her Pyrenean Mountain dog. Doreen, who's the sister-in-law of Marjorie Fawcett, chairman of the Parish Council, is a very small woman and Bruno is a very big dog. The contrast between them once caused Emery Jacobs to say …

"I be surprised she don't pop a saddle on that there dog, and ride him down to the shops."

Bruno settled down on the other side of the bus and watched it carefully as though he thought it might try and escape.

The final animal spectator was Alexis, the African Grey parrot that belongs to Norah Fleming who runs a B&B at the top end of the village. African Greys are very sociable birds and this one tends to go everywhere with Norah, sitting on her shoulder, gently pecking her ear from time to time. Alexis is allowed to fly freely within the house which occasionally causes consternation to a B&B guest, but out of doors he rarely strays far from Norah.

Alexis is quite a character in the village. He can whistle the theme tune to *Eastenders* and he can also make a sound like an electric tin opener which Norah's cats associate with mealtimes. When Alexis makes that noise the cats come running in a fruitless search for food. Alexis sits there watching them, then gives the African Grey version of a chuckle.

Like most African Greys, Alexis has a reasonable vocabulary, reasonable for a parrot anyway. When Norah and Alexis arrived at the bridge, Alexis took off from Norah's shoulder, flew across to the bus, perched on one of the windscreen wipers and said, very loudly and clearly, "Silly Billy."

As an observation on the situation it was no doubt accurate but I don't think the bus driver took much comfort from it.

So, picture the scene. Bus jammed on bridge, cat on parapet gazing fixedly at it, Bruno the Pyrenean Mountain dog keeping guard on the other side and Alexis the African Grey parrot perched on a windscreen wiper peering in.

I can't remember who actually took the shot but a photo

showing the bus surrounded by this trio of animals appeared in the next issue of *The Spyglass,* our village magazine, causing most people, excluding those who had actually been on the bus, to go … "Ahhhh!"

And that was the launch pad for the *Pretty Pets Photo Competition.*

It was Phoebe Jones who came up with the idea. Phoebe and Jasper run the village shop and they have two golden retrievers called Butch and Sundance. Phoebe also has a white cockatoo called Esmeralda.

Phoebe was very taken with the picture of the cat, the dog and the parrot grouped round the stranded bus so she had a word with Marueen Argent who edits *The Spyglass.*

This magazine is the only reliable way of sharing information round the village. True, there is a notice board outside the village hall but that is the other side of the river and you have to make a special journey to look at it. Anyway some people view the notice board with distrust. It is not updated regularly and there is also the problem of it being misused and attracting spurious adverts. A few years ago there was a huge uproar when a notice appeared on the board offering *French Polishing – evenings only.* The next Parish Council meeting was very lively with people shouting "We all know what 'French Polishing' means. We don't want this kind of muck in our village."

The Parish Council promised to investigate which they did and discovered that the person who had posted the advert did genuinely offer French polishing services but as he had a day job he could only meet customers in the evenings.

The Spyglass, under the watchful eye of Maureen, poses

no such risk. Woe betide anyone who gets on the wrong side of Maureen, but she's very good at what she does. In a village where nothing much ever happens Maureen does a sterling job in filling a 20-page magazine once a month.

Anyway, Phoebe spoke to Maureen and suggested that the village ran a *Pretty Pets Photo Competition* with the winning pictures being published in *The Spyglass*.

This conversation, like most significant conversations in my Village in the Valley, took place in The Spy and, again as usual, soon involved everyone in the bar, not just Maureen and Phoebe.

The idea of a pets photo competition met with a lot of enthusiasm but as usual the devil was in the detail. What sort of rules would the competition have? How many entries per person? Who would we get to judge it?

An early suggestion that we should beef it up a bit by making it a *Pets In Costume* competition was quickly kicked into touch, mostly on the grounds of cruelty to the animals but also because it would automatically exclude a lot of pets.

As Marjorie put it, "My granddaughter's pet is a goldfish. Well, you can hardly put a costume on that, can you?"

The simplest option was simply to make it a *Pretty Pets Photo Competition* but we knew from the outset that we'd be faced with umpteen dogs with bows sitting smugly on silk cushions and kittens rolling upside down playing with a ball of wool. The prospect was not appealing so we decided if we were going to do this we'd need an angle.

In the end it was Jessica who cracked it. "If the inspiration for this idea came from that picture of the animals round the stranded bus then why don't we call it *Pets In Odd Poses*," she said. "That picture did rather give the impression that the parrot thought he could have driven the bus better than the driver and if you'd seen Hugo's spaniel doing what I saw Hugo's spaniel doing the other day you'd already have a clear winner with no argument."

Suddenly a piercing female voice rose above the general clamour. "Well, I can tell you this for free, you're not doing that in my kitchen."

We all glanced at each other. The kitchen didn't seem a likely place for pet photography anyway but then we realised this was a totally unconnected conversation happening between a visiting couple on the far side of the bar. The woman suddenly realised that she had spoken louder than intended and turned back to her companion. "Well, not on a Thursday anyway," she said rather more quietly.

There seemed no courteous way of trying to delve deeper into those remarks, tempting though it was to do so. Instead we turned back to the question of the photo competition.

The next question was what constituted a pet. Dogs, cats, birds and what vets refer to as '*small furries*' were clearly not controversial but did a chicken count as a pet if it were only kept for sentimental reasons when its egg laying days were over? And what about silkworms or land snails or rats?

For most people in the village rats are something to be poisoned or shot so, although we realised that white rats could be kept as pets, there wasn't a great deal of enthusiasm for including them.

This argument ranged for some time until Bill cut the gordian knot. "Is there anyone we know in the village who has a pet white rat?" he asked.

We did a quick calculation and came to the answer, "No."

"Then why the hell are we bothering to discuss it?" said Bill, logical as ever.

And so it was decided. The competition would be for *Pets In Odd Poses*, not more than two entries per person, photos had to be printed so they could be displayed at the village hall where the judging would take place.

Hugo Framlingham, chairman of the village hall committee, is a keen photographer but when he was approached and asked if he would judge the competition he refused outright.

"Not on your life. Judge a competition between my friends and neighbours? No way. Bound to upset someone."

Instead he suggested Verity Reddick, a professional photographer in our local market town. When asked, she was only too willing to do the job in return for a free advert in **The Spyglass.**

The announcement of the competition, together with the rules, was laid out in *The Spyglass* and Maureen waited for the entries to come in. Well, they did come in, but there was a snag.

Those of us in The Spy that day when we were deciding on the structure of the competition were all, how shall I put it, of a certain generation. It never occurred to us to ban the use of computerised photo software but that had clearly been the first thought of a number of the younger enthusiastic photographers.

Of course, whatever the stated object of the competition we still got some fluffy kittens doing Houdini tricks with wool and dogs wearing bows that most of them were keen to remove as quickly as possible, but some of the other entries came as a great surprise.

I, myself, am not very skilled with computer photo software. I can take a digital image, re-size it, even crop it if I've got the refuse bin or a pile of ironing in shot, but that's about my limit. Of course I know that skilled operators can do far more than that but we had not expected this in a village photo competition.

However, once we'd got over the shock we did marvel at the ingenuity involved, not just the technical skill but the imagination as well. It's not everyday you see a guinea pig playing football or a canary using a machine gun, let alone a tortoise on roller skates overtaking a rabbit on crutches.

The entries obviously came as a surprise to Verity as well. She had a quiet word with Maureen and Phoebe and asked why *'photo manipulation'* had not been forbidden. They hummed and hawed a bit and then confessed that it hadn't even occurred to them. Verity pointed out that it made her job rather difficult, was she judging photographic skill or computer skill?

"Definitely photographic skill," said Phoebe.

"Well, I agree," said Verity, "but that only constitutes about a third of the entries."

The dilemma was taken to the usual discussion forum in the main bar in The Spy where Bill, who had been fascinated by some of the more imaginative manipulations, came up with the obvious answer.

"Two categories," he said, "traditional photography and electronic manipulation."

And so that's what happened.

All the photos were sent to Verity in advance so she could

consider them at leisure. Then they were printed and pinned up on the walls of the village hall. On the day the results were to be announced we were all invited to go to the hall, examine the photos and then vote for '*The Village Choice*' which might not be the same as the professional judge's choice. It wasn't.

Of course the downside to all of this was that if you are going to choose a winner of anything then, by definition, there will also be a lot of losers. We have had bitter experience of this in the *Village Garden Show* where on occasions there have been fruit and vegetables hurled across the room.

We thought it unlikely that anyone would start throwing cameras about but it is best to be prepared for anything which is why, with hindsight, the village hall committee should never have gone along with Phoebe's last minute suggestion that people could bring the pets they'd photographed along to the hall when the judging was taking place.

You'd think they would have known better.

All went well at first. First prize for a real photo went to Samantha Bracebridge with a shot of her greyhound, Ariadne, lying on her back with all four legs pointing vertically skywards in perfect alignment. Not the usual view of a greyhound. The electronic manipulation category was won by Naomi, Marjorie Fawcett's granddaughter, with her picture of her tortoise, Razzmatazz, climbing up the side of the Eiffel Tower.

The village vote went to Nan Mildew predictably for her kitten in her sewing basket while Susan Forest, the parish clerk won the electronic category for an image of her rabbit entitled '*Dracula*'.

"I wouldn't want a rabbit with teeth like that loose

amongst my carrots," muttered Emery Jacobs.

The pets which had been brought to the hall inevitably included a number of dogs, all on leads and all perfectly well behaved. There were also several cats sulking in a variety of cat carriers. Judging by the number of well clawed forearms on show we assumed that none of the cats had come quietly.

Alexis, the African Grey parrot, was there of course, together with Esmeralda, the white cockatoo. The two birds eyed each other cautiously then Alexis broke the silence.

"Tasty," he remarked but whether he was complimenting Esmeralda on her beautiful white feathers or whether he was making a judgement on her as a potential meal, none of us were sure.

Of course there were escapes. That had always been inevitable. A rabbit was the first to go. It went haring across the hall with every dog in the room straining at its leash to get after it. Fortunately the rabbit ran into the gents toilet where it was easily cornered.

The budgie belonging to Clara Evans was next. It flew around for a while and then landed on one of the rafters and was only re-captured with the aid of a butterfly net – normally used for rescuing stray dragonflies. Then it was a cat who took refuge on top of the kitchen cupboards and was only coaxed down when Sylvia offered it the innards of a fish paste sandwich.

Once the winners had been announced, applause given, disappointed murmurs had died down, Verity had one last surprise for us.

"There was one video entry," she said, "and although it didn't qualify for a prize in either category it is well worth seeing. Ladies and gentlemen, I give you Coriander Sanderson and Hamlet."

She made a signal to Rupert, the lights went out, a projector was started and a picture appeared on the large end wall of the room. It showed a guinea pig – presumably Hamlet – in a cage. The animal was mostly light brown but with white fur round its neck as though it were wearing a ruff. Then Coriander appeared on the edge of frame holding what we were later told was a stick of chicory. The moment Hamlet saw the chicory it began uttering frantic squeaks like a faulty fire alarm.

As we watched, Coriander opened the cage door and offered the stick of chicory towards Hamlet. The guinea pig's mouth opened, there was a continuous crunching sound and the stick of chicory vanished into its jaws like a plank into a buzz saw. As that one disappeared Coriander produced another stick which was rapidly absorbed in the same way. The whole video was accompanied by a rendition of *The Flight of the Bumblebee* on the piano. When the final stick of chicory had vanished into Hamlet's maw, Coriander shut the cage door and the music came to an end. It was magnificent.

As the enthusiastic applause died away Emery Jacobs began singing in a rather quavery voice.

> *How can a Guinea Pig show it's pleased*
> *If it hasn't got a tail to wag?*
> *All other animals you will find*
> *Have got a little tail stuck on behind.*
> *If they'd only put a tail on a guinea pig*
> *And finish off a perfect job,*

> *Then the price of a guinea pig would go right up*
> *From a guinea up to thirty-bob.*

It was another grand performance and elicited yet another round of applause, though several of the younger people present asked in mystification, "What does thirty bob mean?"

When it was explained to them that a bob was a shilling and a guinea was twenty-one shillings in old money – one pound, one shilling – with the added information that things like legal costs used to be stated in guineas, most people under fifty sighed deeply and raised an eyebrow. Clearly the metric generation was not impressed.

The afternoon ended in a typical way for my Village in the Valley. In a moment of quiet we suddenly heard a loud buzzing whining noise and suddenly all the cats in the room began howling.

We looked round to see Alexis sitting innocently on Norah's shoulder and giving the African Grey equivalent of a chuckle.

Clearly Norah's cats were not the only ones to recognise the sound of an electric tin opener.

MORE CANDLES
THAN CAKE

There's an old saying which goes, "*The trouble with the unexpected is that it happens when you least expect it*". That's very true but in my Village in the Valley we've adapted it slightly to say, "*Expect the unexpected*". We've learned that if we do that, we're rarely disappointed.

Thinking about this I am reminded of such occasions as the great denture challenge between Emery Jacobs and Ronald Trigg. It started because Emery had been to Sunday lunch with some friends and during the meal his false teeth had fallen out into the gravy jug. Nothing stays secret for long round here so this episode quickly became known around the village. The younger people thought it was funny, the older ones were sympathetic, all except Ronald Trigg that is. He started poking fun at Emery in The Spy one evening, laughing at him and saying that gravy was all he could manage with no teeth of his own left.

"Or I suppose you could just about slurp down a drop of custard if pushed," he added.

Emery was livid. "I bet I've got more of me own teeth left than you have," he yelled.

"Nonsense," replied Ronald, "most of me teeth are still me own. Just a couple of little gaps here and there which had to be filled."

"Load of old cobblers, my man," said Emery, "the teeth you've got couldn't even chew a slice o' pork unless he were minced up first."

As pork is one of the key industries in our part of the world this amounted to a serious insult and it was Ronalds's turn to be livid.

"I don't have no trouble with pork," he yelled. "Not like you, living on slops 'cos you can't chew."

"That's a lie," responded Emery, "and I'll prove it."

"Then so will I."

While the customers in The Spy watched entranced both men reached into their mouths clearly planning on removing and comparing their respective dentures but then Dan stepped in.

"Oh, no you don't," he said, "I'll not be having any denture wars in my bar. If you want to bite each other, or even gum each other, then you can go outside and not come back."

For most people in my Village in the Valley the prospect of being barred from The Spy is a worse prospect than losing a winning lottery ticket. The Spy is the centre of village life where people meet, talk, drink, find company and no one wants to put that at risk.

There was some mumbling from both Emery and Ronald but the denture exposure threat subsided and tactful friends guided them to opposite ends of the bar for the rest of the evening.

I suppose that sort of behaviour is what you would call eccentric but the other behaviour that's prevalent in my

Village in the Valley is determination.

A good example of that is Mr Osbaldiston. The story goes that he learned to knit when he was in his early seventies but actually that's not quite right. According to Mrs Pettigrew, who sometimes does his shopping for him, Mr Osbaldiston had first learned to knit when he was in his twenties and serving in the navy but once he was discharged he let it drop. For many years his main passion was growing vegetables in his garden but as he got older his back became stiffer and his gardening stints became shorter. These days the most comfortable posture for him is sitting on an upright chair with a firm wooden back. The snag is that he has no patience with daytime television and had never been much of a reader, so he was very bored just sitting there even though he was much more comfortable.

Then he heard that Clara Evans and Nan Mildew were organising a sale of work to raise money for a local orphanage so he decided to take up knitting again. He asked them what kind of thing would be best.

"Almost anything fancy," said Clara.

"Only not tea cosies," said Nan, "no one uses them these days, it's all instant tea bags straight into a mug." She sighed a little. "I never get to use my mother's teacups and saucers any more."

"How about something for the kiddies," said Clara, "knitted toys always go down well."

So Mr Osbaldiston began knitting, sitting in an upright posture on his upright chair and he was surprisingly good. And fast. He had chosen to knit Velociraptors on the grounds that dinosaurs were always popular with children and knitting one was a real challenge. Mr Osbaldiston liked a challenge.

The multi-coloured knitted Velociraptors proved a great success. The trouble was that Mr Osbaldiston was producing them faster than they could be sold. The first batch for the sale of work quickly sold out and soon there wasn't a house in the village that didn't have a knitted Velociraptor on display. Clara, anxious not to seem ungrateful, set about contacting other villages when they had a sale or a fête or indeed any event coming up. That disposed of a good number but the Velociraptors still kept coming.

Clara and Nan tried tactfully to suggest he stopped or at least perhaps try a different design but Mr Osbaldiston wouldn't listen. He was quite happy, he had the Velociraptor pattern down to a fine art, he used to put a disc of Big Band music in his CD player and sit there on his hard backed chair happily knitting away. The only time he stopped was when he had to water his vegetables.

"I said I'd knit," he said, "and knit I will."

Determination.

Then there was the young lass, name escapes me, some relative of Robert and Matilda Blenkinsop I think, who many years ago dropped out of medical school, trained to be a car mechanic and ended up as chief engineer with a Formula 1 racing team. That certainly took determination.

And of course there was the classic example of Old Crested, whose inventions included the sundial that worked at night, the self righting wellington boots and the musical kettle. His efforts were not always well received but he kept going. Determination, you see.

All very impressive, but for my money when you mention *'determination'* the queen of them all is Esme Fritter.

Esme is a widow who lives in a tiny cottage at the top end of the village. She is quite a small lady with a beaming smile, always willing to help at any event or occasion. She usually maintains she can't really do what she's being asked to do, but then goes on and does it and does it well. Then suddenly out of the blue when she was 76 years old she founded *Grannytronics* and if that doesn't show determination, what does?

Esme was not a technophobe. She had a mobile phone and a laptop computer. She could look up information online and she had her own email address. However, apart from that, what she knew about computers and associated matters could be written on the head of a pin using a pneumatic drill.

This didn't really bother her. She had never felt the need for anything else, but then her grand-daughter and her husband, who lived about thirty miles away, well over the county border, announced they were about to have a baby. They were thrilled and Esme was thrilled. She already had three grandchildren and now she was going to be a great-grandmother. Wonderful, but ironically it was this baby that made Esme feel she was inadequate.

Not inadequate about the baby of course. Esme had raised two daughters and a son, to say nothing of helping with three grandchildren and as far as she was concerned the broad principles of childcare had not changed significantly. True, there were now disposable nappies instead of the terry towelling ones that had to be put in a tin bucket with a sterilising solution. True, these days there was a far wider range of baby foods on the market. True, the toys suitable for a small baby were more varied and safer than the ones Esme remembered, though she did wonder if some of the more complex mobiles were more for the amusement of the parents rather than the child. However, in spite of all this, the basics were the same. Cuddle it, feed it, clean it, love it, let it sleep safely – these were the eternals.

About six months after the baby was born she was asked to go over and babysit for a few days as her granddaughter and her husband had to go away for a long weekend. She was delighted and arrived full of expectations but what she hadn't expected was the range of electronic contraptions that now filled the whole house.

Her granddaughter gave her the guided tour.

"It's all quite straightforward, Gran. This is the bottle warmer. It's all programmed for pre-set times so it will chime fifteen minutes before the feed is due and then will go bong when the feed is ready. You only have to reset the timer once a day. As soon as the feed is over, you put the bottle in this machine so it will get cleaned and sterilised, the normal cleaning program is fine for most of the time but once a day use the ultra clean setting. Once that's done you can make up the new feed, put the bottle back in the warmer, press the reset button – that's this one here – and it will automatically go on to the next time setting."

Esme listened with mounting dismay. Her granddaughter went on, explaining how the cat's feeding bowl operated on a timer so that the bowl could be filled at the start of each day, but then four different flaps opened at set intervals thus controlling how much the cat could eat at one time.

"If we give it to her in one go she bolts the lot and throws up over the carpet."

On and on went the list. The electronic doorbell that took pictures of anyone who came to the door, the mobile phone dock with special alarm buttons for different types of emergency, the klaxon hooter that went off if the nursery got too hot or too cold, the toy rabbit beside the cot that was programmed to start playing soothing music if the baby stirred, the video camera that projected an image of the nursery onto a screen in every room in the house including, to Esme's surprise, the toilet.

"So there you go. Got all that, Gran?"

"Yes, dear," said Esme thinking, *cuddle it, feed it, clean it, love it, let it sleep safely.*

"Oh, I should just warn you. The musical rabbit can be a bit flaky. It sometimes plays too loud and sometimes just starts up without any reason and doesn't always play at the right speed. It's a bit of a pain but the baby does love it so we put up with it."

"Don't worry, dear, I'll manage."

"Great. Well, we'd better be off."

"I don't have to plug the baby in to recharge it or anything, do I?" Esme asked mischievously, but her granddaughter was rushing round, gathering up all her bits and pieces and did not hear her.

The weekend, of course, went fine, at least as far as the baby was concerned. The equipment was another matter. The mechanical bottle warmer wouldn't stop bonging, so Esme unplugged it and heated the bottle in a saucepan on the stove as she had always done. The cat's food bowl never seemed to open so she decided when the cat should be fed and put the biscuits down at the appropriate time. As for the musical rabbit, well, it certainly was a law unto itself. If it had been a teenager, Esme thought, she'd have said it had been smoking pot. It was both random and irritating, suddenly starting to play for no apparent reason, usually at very high volume, sometimes slow and sometimes fast. She could not find out how to turn it off so she stuck it in the toilet where it could play music – unheard by her – to the baby on the video monitor screen.

When they got home she tried to explain about the various technical problems but, although her granddaughter was grateful for the baby sitting, she had no patience with Esme's technical incompetence.

"Oh, Gran, please. This is the 21st century."

Esme smiled, but inwardly she was saying, *cuddle it, feed it, clean it, love it, let it sleep safely.*

A few days later Esme was having coffee with a couple of friends in a café in the nearby market town and she told them all about the gadgets in her granddaughter's house.

"Load of old cobblers. I can't be doing with all that caper," said the man, "old fogies like us can't be expected to understand all this computer stuff."

"Well, I suppose some men can," said his wife, "but obviously women will never manage it."

Esme was fond of them both but found their attitude very hard to take.

"I'm not an old fogey," she thought, "and I certainly don't accept that a man might be able to cope with technical things but not a woman. That's insulting."

The next trigger that led to *Grannytronics* was a letter in the local press from an elderly man who had missed his train because the station no longer had a ticket office staffed by humans and he could not understand how the automatic ticket machine worked.

Then she heard about a lady who had received a fine for not paying a parking charge in a car park where the only payment option was by a mobile phone. The lady in question could not read the instructions which were in very tiny print so she could not pay.

Esme began exploring this situation of the elderly versus technology and learned about several other problems. A key one was of people who had ordered things online but when they arrived they were the wrong item or the wrong size. All the sellers offered a return option but some of them insisted on this being done through a QR code which many older people simply did not understand.

She thought long and hard about all these incidents and finally decided that there was a problem here that needed to be addressed. Clearly the world was becoming increasingly automatic and electronic and that was not going to change.

So if that's the case it's us who have to change, thought Esme, *whether we like it or not.*

She went online – she had no problem with doing that – and ordered a self-published book called *Simple Explanations for the Technically Challenged*. She read the first three chapters and came to the conclusion that the writer was the one who was technically challenged. The book was full of incomprehensible explanations and spelling mistakes.

This is a waste of time, she thought. *What I need is someone to give me a practical guide on how the technology behind all these gadgets works.*

The trouble was that most of her friends were in the same age bracket as her and knew as little as she did. Obviously she needed someone younger, but who? Then she had a thought. She remembered that when there had been all that trouble with the church clock not striking properly someone had come up with a computer solution.

She couldn't remember who it had been but when she mentioned it to Sunita Devi, Sunita knew.

Oh, that was Bill," she said, "you know, the man who used to be in the army. Has that great big workshop in his garden. His wife calls it his playroom."

A few days later Esme happened to be in the village shop when Bill came in. Rather diffidently she asked him how he had dealt with the problems of the church clock.

"Ah, yes, the clock," he said, "that was a bit of a challenge. I was certainly involved but it was Logan who was the brains behind it."

"Logan?"

"Yes, he's the grandson of Dan and Maureen Argent at The Spy. He's only 13 but he's a real technical whizz."

Esme wasn't a great one for the pub but that evening she went into The Spy and asked Dan if he could spare a minute.

"Sure," he said, "what's up?"

"I was wondering if I could borrow your grandson," said Esme, "I need some computer advice. I'll pay him, of course," she added.

Dan scratched his head. "No harm in asking him," he said, "teenage lads can always use a bit of extra pocket money.

He'll be over here on Sunday. Shall I fix up a meeting?"

"Yes please."

So the following Sunday Esme, 76, met Logan, 13, and in spite of the age difference they bonded instantly. Logan thought her idea was brilliant so they sat down and began mapping out the main areas that Esme needed to understand.

"I don't need a huge amount of detail," she said, "what people need to know is how to do various things on their computer, their tablet, their phone or their smart TV, but also to understand the broad principles behind what they're doing so if they come across something different they can reason it through for themselves."

"Cool," said Logan.

And so this unlikely partnership began. Every Sunday Logan would visit his grandparents then after lunch he'd trot up to the top end of the village and he and Esme would explore another area of modern technology. The first thing Logan showed her was how to download and use a recording device on her mobile phone so she could record everything he told her, then play it back and transcribe it at her leisure.

Somehow Logan had the knack of explaining things in terms she readily understood and soon things like WhatsApp, QR codes, managing electronic car park and railway ticket machines, Instagram, FaceTime, Google Maps, streaming and so on were no longer a mystery to her.

It took a long time but, with a lot of determination on her part and a lot of patience from Logan, she eventually felt confident that there wasn't much she didn't understand or could at least reason out. Logan paid her the ultimate compliment.

"You know what, Mrs Fritter, I reckon you're an honorary teenager."

She was very moved.

Having acquired all this knowledge and skill Esme decided it was time to share it with others like her so she began advertising in the local area.

Struggling with modern technology? Come to 'Grannytronics' and learn the basics

She rented the village hall for a morning each week and ran a kind of technical surgery. From the outset she realised that it had to be one-to-one sessions just as she had had from Logan. Different people had different needs. One person was fine with Facebook but struggled to pay in a car park, another was quite at home with a video call but could not get their head round QR codes. She made a nominal charge for each person, enough to cover the cost of hiring the hall and her sessions were soon oversubscribed. Before long, people started bringing cakes and biscuits and the session developed into a kind of technical coffee morning.

Having got that running Esme decided that the next stage was to draft a simple guidebook explaining the main points about modern technology that elderly people needed to know. She wrote the text herself but went through it with Logan who made a few suggestions. She listened carefully to him, made a few changes but did not accept all his ideas. Logan's vocabulary and the vocabulary of her target audience did not always coincide. She did, however, give him a credit. She thought that was the least he deserved.

She called the book *New Tech for Old Timers* by Esme Fritter, technical consultant Logan Argent, copyright *Grannytronics*. She self-published it online (having checked the spelling carefully) and before long she had sold several hundred copies.

Word gets around in small communities, especially in my Village in the Valley, so the next thing that happened was that Esme was invited to appear on the morning show at the local radio station.

She was a gift to the interviewer. She knew exactly what she wanted to say and spoke well and clearly. She hammered home the point that much modern technology discriminated against the elderly but the determined elderly were prepared to fight back. There was only one slight hiccup and even that worked to her advantage.

"Well, thank you, Mrs Fritter," said the interviewer, "I must say you've shown a lot of initiative getting *Grannytronics* off the ground. As you say, we do tend to think of computers and technology as being a young person thing and yet you've proved the opposite. Would it be indiscreet to ask how old you are?"

"Yes, it would be indiscreet," said Esme, "all I'll say is that when my birthday comes round there are more candles than cake these days."

The rollercoaster rolled on. Esme was a guest on the regional television programme, she was invited to speak at the local Rotary Club, U3A and Probus. She began getting letters from elderly people all over the country thanking her for making their technical lives easier.

"I beat the machine at our local railway station," wrote

one lady, "I not only got my ticket out of the damn thing, I managed to help a young man when he got confused."

"I'm much happier ordering things online now," wrote an 80 year old man, "now I understand these funny little codes I can send it all back when I don't like it."

"Thank you so much," wrote a couple both in their nineties. "Using your guide we have managed to set up a video link to our family in Australia so at last we can see and speak to our grandchildren properly."

Esme was quietly pleased with the success of *Grannytronics* but to her mind her greatest achievement was more local. Over the last few sessions she had had with Logan she had asked him to concentrate on a very specific problem. At first he had thought she was potty but she explained the background so, as they had become good friends, he did what she asked.

The outcome was that next time she visited her granddaughter she took her tool kit with her, dismantled the musical rabbit, found out where the intermittent fault was, replaced two capacitors and left it working properly.

Her granddaughter was speechless.

If You Believe In Fairies Clap Your Hands

A year in the life of a village is often marked by certain milestones. Some villages have fetes, we have a carnival. We also have an Easter Egg hunt, a charity raft race, a summer barbecue and a garden show. However the climax of our year is definitely the village pantomime.

This event splits the local population into two groups. First there are those who have no ambition to strut the boards wearing unsuitable clothes and making a prat of themselves but are very happy to come along, cheer, boo and clap as appropriate. Second are those who would kill for a chance to be in it, to have their moment of glory in a fashion far removed from everyday life.

They pay no heed to Old Falstaff sitting by the fire in The Spy when he says – as he always does at panto time.

> *"Life's but a walking shadow, a poor player*
> *That struts and frets his hour upon the stage*
> *And then is heard no more."*

Inevitably someone in the bar will then say, "Isn't that from …?"

Whereupon Jessica leaps in with, "Don't say the name.

It's from The Scottish Play. Don't jinx the pantomime."

People in the second group tend not to worry about "being heard no more" and there is never any shortage of people wanting a part.

I've noticed over the years that once someone has been cast they tend to assume the characteristics of the person they are playing for the duration of the event. This can sometimes result in some interesting situations.

Stick a pair of tights on people and persuade them to yell "He's behind you …" "Oh, no he isn't …" and suddenly quiet, well mannered people are pushing others out of the way and demanding to be served first in the village pub.

Dan, the landlord of The Spy, always goes on high alert from around mid-November, unless he is in the cast himself in which case he is the one shouting the loudest and trying to slide whiskey glasses along the bar in real Wild West fashion. He's not very good at it and they usually end up on the floor much to the annoyance of his wife, Maureen.

It's a serious business, the village pantomime.

This particular year was even more interesting. When the pantomime committee, which is basically just a group of us who meet in The Spy, got together we decided that Jessica should direct the show this year. Our reasoning was that she had worked in television and had experience in directing small scale theatre productions and you can't get much more small scale than our village hall.

It's not a large building, our village hall. Basically it is one large room with a kitchen, loos and a couple of small meeting rooms off to one side. The hall itself can seat around 60 people so long as they don't mind being cosy. It has a small raised stage at one end but none of the fancy bits and pieces you associate with a theatre so any performance has to be carefully tailored to the space available.

Having chosen our director we turned to the question of what pantomime we should do. Last year we had done a version of *Sleeping Beauty*. The Princess was played by Susan Forest, our Parish Clerk, but our local odd job man, Matt Cookham, who played the Prince, got a bit over enthusiastic when waking her with a kiss. There are many different versions of *Sleeping Beauty* but as far as we know none of them have the line:

If you put your hand there again, mate, I'll clock you round the head with a claw hammer.

When it comes to the actual script we always prefer to write our own, though sticking to the broad outline of whatever traditional panto we've chosen. That way we can incorporate lots of local references, tweak the available parts to those in the village who are actually available and make sure that the action can be accommodated in a small space. There's no scope for large scale song and dance numbers in our hall.

Initially Jessica said she wanted to write the script as well as direct it which, on the surface, seemed a good idea. However, her first suggestions didn't quite fit the concept of a village pantomime. One of her ideas was to do *Jack and The Beanstalk* from the point of view of the Ogre. In Jessica's proposed version the Ogre was a kindly old man minding his own business until teenage hooligan Jack and his band of tearaways came climbing up the beanstalk bent on mayhem and with their eyes on the Ogre's treasure. Very avant-garde but possibly not average village hall material.

Her next idea was to do what she called '*a reverse Cinderella*'. In this version Cinderella was a money grabbing harpy, determined to kick her sisters out of the way, grab the Prince, marry him for his money then abandon all of them for a life of self-indulgent luxury.

Bearing in mind that our village panto always attracted a lot of children in the audience this didn't seem like such a good idea either so we persuaded Jessica that she could do a better job of directing if she was working with someone else's script.

At this point Harry and Sylvia stepped forward. We had a moment's hesitation wondering what might emerge from a collaboration between a retired merchant banker and the widow of a dentist, but we reasoned that it couldn't be any worse than a version of *Dick Whittington* where the cat is sacrificed to the sun god as Dick approaches London (another Jessica suggestion). In any case it's always hard to turn down willing volunteers so Harry and Sylvia got the gig.

They went away to talk about it and at our next meeting announced they had decided to do *Babes In The Wood*. Jessica objected on the grounds that working with child actors, especially amateur ones, was never going to be easy but we pointed out to her that this was a village pantomime. So long as the Babes were fairly obviously under 30, no one was going to quibble.

The first surprise was when Sylvia and Harry delivered the script. They had chosen to present it in verse, rhyming couplets to be precise. Initially there were a few raised eyebrows but once we'd had a bit of a read through it became apparent that couplets with a rhythm and a rhyme were much easier to learn.

You can tweak most pantomimes to suit the people and facilities available and our version of *Babes In The Wood* was no exception. The thrust of the story was that Baron Bluenose and his wife were on their uppers. Noble name, big house, but no dosh, a fact made clear by their faithful old retainer Roderick at the very beginning of the pantomime.

RODERICK: *O Baron Bluenose, master mine,*
Alack a day, we have no wine.
We have no bread, we have no meat,
We haven't got a thing to eat.
The dog is dying, the cat is dead,
The grooms cannot get up from bed
Because their livery has been pawned.
Master, our last day has dawned.
We have reached our last resources,
Unless, of course, we eat the horses.

So, the Bluenoses are already in dire straights and on top of that they learn that the Baron's brother, Rupert, has just died. A moment's hope. Has he left them his money? Of course he hasn't, he's left it all to his two children and to add insult to injury he's appointed Baron Bluenose as their guardian. That's two more mouths to feed. Crisis. But wait, the Baron has a solution. Bump off the kids and Rupert's money will come to them.

BARON: *If we're to live the kids must die,*
You want to live and so do I.
The two little kids
Have got the quids
Get rid of the kids,
We get the quids.
Simples.

Having taken the decision to dispose of his niece and nephew the Baron recruits the villain, the dastardly Deadly Dan, to remove the Babes from the land of the living. While the two of them are engaged in plotting, the Baroness, who is secretly in love with Roderick their faithful servant, realises that she can't stand her husband any more so she and Roderick plan to run away together.

BARONESS: *Roderick dear I'd have you kiss me,*
Don't shut your eyes or else you'll miss me

RODERICK: *O my love, my life, my queen,*
We'll buy a house in Bethnal Green
We'll have a dog, yes, and a cat,
And 'welcome' written on the mat.
We'll have a garden full of pansies
And water them with water cansies.

So far, so good. Traditional pantomime stuff, but then in Act 2 Harry and Sylvia departed from the usual plot and quite unashamedly went for laughs by creating a bunch of unconventional fairies who would save the Babes. They explained their thinking to Jessica who blinked a bit but gradually realised that their idea could be the making of the show. And, as it turned out, it certainly was.

So Act 2 opens with the arrival of Maymorn, the fairy queen, and her fairy band. This spritely mafia are visited by the ghost of the Baron's brother, Rupert, who tells the fairies about the dastardly plan being hatched by Baron Bluenose and Deadly Dan to dispose of his two sweet little children – the Babes – so they can get their hands on the kids' inheritance.

The fairies swing into action, the Baron and Deadly Dan get their comeuppance, the Baroness and Roderick run off together and everyone – or everyone still alive – lives happily ever after.

Having got a script the next stage was the casting. Nigel Grayling was a shoo in for Baron Bluenose. Nigel was delighted to have such a central part but less happy with the assumption that, as a one-time solicitor, he would be only too familiar with dirty deeds aimed at appropriating someone else's money. Marjorie Fawcett, the Parish Council chairman, was Baroness Bluenose and Jasper Jones from the village shop was Roderick, their faithful old retainer.

Jasper loved the idea of having a fling with the chairman of the Parish Council and we could all see that in a way Marjorie was quite chuffed at the idea of having a fictional affair. However, she made it clear that, whichever way the script developed, kissing was not on the agenda. We all got the impression that Jasper was quite relieved at that.

The next decision was who would play the villain, the dastardly Deadly Dan. The first suggestion for this part – purely because of the name – was Dan Argent from The Spy, but he declined. He and Maureen had seven grandchildren who would be coming to the performance and they thought that seeing their grandad planning to bump off a couple of kids would not go down well.

The next choice was Humphrey Snape, captain of the bell ringing team. He was a bachelor, a misogynist and a pretty grumpy bloke all round. The idea of bumping off the Babes didn't worry him at all. All he wanted was the chance to wear a twirly moustache and to say things like '*Gadzooks*' from time to time.

Harry and Sylvia said that '*Gadzooks*' would have to be negotiated but we could all see Humphrey's suitability for the role. As Nigel put it, "He's a dead ringer for a baddie." There was a chorus of groans.

However, Harry and Sylvia had no intention of portraying on-stage murder in the village pantomime. It would definitely happen off stage and would not involve direct violence. So in their script Deadly Dan comes up with a plan.

DEADLY DAN: *I have a scheme that's slow but sure,*
A plan that's free from muck and gore.
So here's my plan, it's rather good,
I'll lose the kids in a local wood.
There alone, in dark privation,
They'll die of famine and starvation.
My hands will then be free from blood,
My reputation free from mud.
Gadzooks.

A dastardly plot, emphasised by Humphrey's over-the-top moustache twirling. The innocent Babes were played by Ashley, aged 22, son of Norah and Jack Fleming who run a local B&B and farm shop and Marilyn, aged 28 daughter of Roger Fraser, one of the local farmers. Ashley and Marilyn had great fun, especially as the Babes in Harry and Sylvia's version aren't the most tactful of children. When George and Joan first arrive at Bluenose castle the Baroness tries to comfort them for the loss of their Dad. Turns out that's not necessary.

GEORGE: *They buried our father yesterday,*
Above him clouds were dark and grey.
Things were quiet and O so still
Until we found the old boy's will,
And then we both went on the spree
He'd left it all to Joan and me.

JOAN: *We'll go to Monte Carlo,*
And see Vienna too.
We'll see the Sphinx and Pyramids
And go to Timbuctoo.

GEORGE: *We'll live on jam and caviar*
Oysters and marmalade
We'll buy a stall in the market place
And do a roaring trade.

BARON: *Yes, yes, dear children, now if you're good*
My friend will take you to a wood.

> *A wood that's green and very fair is,*
> *And full of pixies, gnomes and fairies.*

DEADLY DAN: [aside] *The dirty deed will soon be done,*
These kids, their useful course have run.

JOAN: *I want to see the gnomes and pixies*
Remember now, no dirty tricksies

Even so, it seems the Babes are doomed and their imminent demise brings Act 1 to a close.

It is in Act 2 that everything really takes off. The curtain rises – well actually we don't have a curtain so while everyone is drinking tea and knocking back sausage rolls in one of the meeting rooms, those of us who were roped in as stage crew were busy dismantling the painted backdrop that had been Bluenose Castle and erecting two cardboard trees in their place.

The opening scene is set in the Forest of Fewtreeze and to the accompaniment of Pawel playing a lively flourish on his ukelele, Maymorn, the Fairy Queen makes her entrance.

MAYMORN: *I am Maymorn, of fairies queen,*
Tra-la, I dance o'er the verdant green.
Come my subject hear my call,
Treading lightly, one and all.
Daybreak, Daybreak. Where art thou?
Twilight, Twilight. Gone where now?
And where are you sweet Rainyday,
Have goblins stole thy love away?

Gossamer, will you answer me.
Have you now no loyalty?
Are you courting with some gnome?
Is it washing day at home?

After a bit of arm twisting, and a promise that no kissing was involved, Susan Forrest was persuaded to take the part of Maymorn. She looked very fetching in silvery tights, a pair of gossamer wings and a wand with a star on its tip.

But it was the casting of Maymorn's four fairies that was the triumph of the show. All of them were male and not one of them under sixty years old.

The first fairy, Daybreak, was played by Emery Jacobs

DAYBREAK: *I am Daybreak, light and airy,*
On the whole a nice, kind fairy.
It is I, who at dawn goeth,
To make each cock, its hoarse crow croweth.
I steep the world in dew at dawn.
And tell the sun to rise each morn.

Then came Twilight played by Ronald Trigg.

TWILIGHT: *I was born in sombre hours,*
When wizards practise awful powers.
When cat creeps off with death-trapped mouse,
And lights are lit in every house.
The twinkling stars proclaim my fame
Twilight is my pretty name.

Newton Flotman, otherwise known as Old Crested, played Rainyday.

RAINYDAY: *I am called sweet Rainyday.*
Born in April so they say.
I make the sunshine twixt the showers,
And create the storm-born hours,
Spit and splutter
In the gutter.
When it's raining,
I am reigning.
Campers hate me,
Hikers berate me,
I am Rainyday.

But the star of the fairy ring was undoubtedly Gossamer played by Silas Pring, the cowman on the Blenkinsop farm.

GOSSAMER: *I was born in a buttercup,*
Tra-la, Tra-la.
Born as the sun came stealing up,
Tra-la, Tra-la.
The beetles and frogs came creeping near.
"Oh look," they cried, "there's a fairy here."
And the noise they made was O so great,
It reached the Queen, where she sat in state.
And hastening quick, she came to me,
Where I lay beneath the greenwood tree.
Gossamer she called me when she came,
And Gossamer is my fairy name.

Tra-la, Tra-la,
My man.

We never really discovered how Jessica had manged to persuade four elderly men to wear silver wings, a sparkling bodice, a fluffed out tutu and make prats of themselves in front of their neighbours. Rumour has it that it involved a sizable amount of beer money behind the bar in The Spy and the promise of a feature article in the local paper. However, whatever she promised them they all agreed and once it became clear that they would be the highlight of the show they all threw themselves into the roles enthusiastically.

And no one was disappointed. The line-up of elderly fairies stole the show. Those of us who'd had a preview at the dress rehearsal waited with anticipation for the audience reaction on the night and we were not disappointed. When they first appeared Bev the Rev laughed so loudly that she spilt her lime juice straight down her front.

MAYMORN: *The sun that rose in beauty sets apace,*
And night in twilight shows its darkling face.
Sleep will encircle this our beauteous wood.
Don't interrupt me, subjects, this stuff's good.

RAINYDAY: *Get a move on Queenie,*
Cut the long words out,
I'm standing here half naked,
I want to move about.

TWILIGHT: *My feet are cold, my legs are hairy.*
I don't wanna be a fairy.

MAYMORN: *The grass is soft like Twilights head.*
To us the weary world is dead.
Let us forget this life of woe,
Let's trip the light fantastic toe.

DAYBREAK: *Queen, you're weak in the top-attic,*
I can't dance my backs rheumatic.

RAINYDAY: *Queen, give this fact your attention.*
I soon will draw my old age pension.

GOSSAMER: *Dancing I also have my qualms,*
I'm paralysed in both my arms.

The plot proceeds when the ghost of Rupert, father of the Babes, learns about the dastardly plan to dispose of his children and enlists the aid of the fairies of the forest to come to their rescue.

GHOST: *I fear my brother, Marmaduke*
Has earned a well deserved rebuke.
The cunning, lying crafty hound
Will kill my kids, that I'll be bound.
And as I have but ghostly brains
And ghostly blood runs in my veins
I can do nothing. Woe is me
Who'll help a ghost in misery?

MAYMORN: *Subjects, someone needs our aid.*
Will your Queen now be obeyed?
Will you help put matters straight
And save these children from their fate?

GOSSAMER: *Count on me ...*

DAYBREAK: *And me as well.*

RAINYDAY: *I'll save the boy ...*

TWILIGHT: [Suggestively] *... and I the gel.*

The first part of the panto had been received with rapturous applause but it was the fairies in the second half that cemented this evening into the collective memory of the village. And not just for the incongruity of the actors either, for even elderly male fairies with hairy legs can get upstaged and towards the end of the second half there was an unscheduled change of script.

The fairies were in the process of confronting Deadly Dan and rescuing the Babes when the village hall door was flung open and Tom Riley rushed into the room. Tom is a local policeman and his message was clear.

"There's a bunch of cows escaped. They're blocking the road."

As the only cows in the area were the pedigree herd belonging to Robert Blenkinsop and as the Blenkinsop cowman, Silas Pring, was on the stage at the time, there was no doubt about the next move. Abandoning his role as Fairy Gossamer, Silas leapt off the stage, his frilly tutu billowing out round him and headed for the door. He was closely followed by Fairy Daybreak (Emery Jacobs) and Fairy Twilight (Ronald Twigg), both of them also used to handling livestock. Fairy Rainyday (Old Crested) stayed put, his experience being more with mechanical contrivances than anything on four legs.

Everyone else piled out after them as clearly there was an even better show going on outside.

On the deserted stage Fairy Rainyday looked at Maymorn, the Fairy Queen, and said, "Well, if we're the only two left, d'you fancy a kiss?"

Susan Forest didn't think that was funny.

Once out in the street there was something of an anti-climax. Some of us, mostly the non-farming elements of the village, were expecting to see a stampede of cattle as we'd seen in countless Westerns, charging down the road, kicking everything aside as they went. Instead there were around eight cows wandering peacefully along past the pub. They obviously weren't a danger to anyone but they were valuable animals and were totally ignoring the traffic building up in front and behind them.

They clearly needed corralling – as John Wayne might have said – but fortunately Silas was up for the challenge.

He held up a warning hand to stop those of us behind him rushing forward. "Don't spook them," he said, "leave this to me."

Emery Jacobs nodded. "Be you going to drive 'em or lead 'em, Silas?" he asked.

"Lead 'em," Silas said, "We be lucky. That's Ermintrude

up front."

Some of us looked puzzled so Ronald Trigg explained. "There's always a lead cow, one that the others will all follow. If Silas controls her, he can lead the others to safety."

"How will he control her?" asked Jessica.

Ronald shrugged his shoulders to make his fairy wings more comfortable and smoothed down his tutu with one hand. "Just you watch."

So we watched as Silas threaded his way through the cows, trying not to let his wings snag on their horns. He gradually edged forward until he was right behind Ermintrude. Once in position he gave her a whack on the bum with his fairy wand, not hard but hard enough to be felt. Ermintrude gave a sort of snort and moved a little way ahead, just enough room for Silas to act. He gripped his wand between his teeth then ran forward, his fairy tutu waving in the breeze and, placing his hands on the cow's bottom, he leapt up onto her back, landing where her saddle would have been if she'd been a horse.

"Yee Ha," muttered Nigel under his breath.

It was certainly an impressive performance. Once established on Ermintrude's back, Silas used his wand to tap her gently and indicate where he wanted her to go. Roger had run ahead and opened the gate to one of his fields so Silas guided Ermintrude through onto the grass with the other seven cows following meekly behind. There they were safely enclosed so we left them there for the night and we all traipsed back to the hall.

By common consent it was decided that the panto was over. The Babes had been rescued. The wicked Baron had got his comeuppance and after Silas's demonstration of rodeo riding anything else would seem an anticlimax.

For the majority of the audience, most of whom were not farmers, Silas was the hero of the hour but he was having none of it.

"Easy job," he said, "even though the timing were bad."

"But what would you have done if they had rampaged though the village," someone asked.

"Rampaged?" said Silas, "Ermintrude don't rampage. She just got bored and went for a walk and the others went with her." He paused for a moment. "I'll need to check the fencing up at High Meadow before we take them back tomorrow."

"Why do you call her Ermintrude?"

Silas shrugged. "Her face reminds me of my old granny. Seemed appropriate."

"Sounds like you're really fond of that cow."

"Well, yes, I do be fond of her. She's a lovely animal and very biddable. Bit too curious for her own good maybe. Mind you," he added, "I'm not too happy with her tonight."

"Because she escaped and interrupted the show?"

"Nah. It's because in all that running and jumping I've only gone an' laddered me tights."

About the Author

Michael Bartlett has been a regular writer for hit programmes for radio and television, and he has also written numerous original plays which have been staged for radio, TV and theatre across the UK. He lives with his wife in Norfolk.

He is the author of short story collections *My Village in the Valley (2021)*, *Personal Islands (2021)*, *A Different Drum (Austin Macauley, 2024)*, and novels *Dreams of Eleven (2022)* and *Hunting the Hornets (2023)*. He returns to the comedy of life in a quiet backwater with short story sequel *Return to My Village in the Valley*.

THE NEW THRILLER

'Gripping from start to finish, once picked up, difficult to put down'

In a world where unscrupulous businessmen, rogues and thieves operate across borders and beyond the reach of the Law, the hope for justice lies with a brilliant former agent known only by a codename. The Hunter.

ISBN 9781915067326

OUT NOW
crumpsbarnstudio.co.uk

If you loved this book, you'll love these other titles from Michael Bartlett:

My Village in the Valley

Discover a quiet unassuming place where, on the whole, very little happens. Until, that is, the community gets together to tackle aggressive drivers, disputed footpaths, yapping hearthrugs and the ubiquitous village fete. The original short story collection My Village in the Valley, where nothing is ever simple ...

ISBN 9781915067005

Personal Islands

Solitude can mean freedom. Or it can mean being in a crowd and knowing how impossible it is to truly share another's thoughts. Original and compelling, this short story collection is an intimate study of the human experience of isolation

ISBN 9781838229894

Dreams of Eleven

When Richard announces he's looking for Julie, a girl he last saw 40 years ago, everyone suspects he's still carrying a torch for his childhood sweetheart. But this search is so much more. The stunning debut novel from Michael Bartlett

ISBN 9781915067173

Crumps Barn Studio
www.crumpsbarnstudio.co.uk